My Secret Unicorn

Flying High

and

Starlight Surprise

Linda Chapman

Illustrated by Biz Hull

PUFFIN

PUFFIN BOOKS

Penguin Books Ltd, 80 Strand, London WC2R ORL, England
Penguin Group (USA) Inc., 375 Hudson Street, New York, New York 10014, USA
Penguin Group (Canada), 10 Alcorn Avenue, Toronto, Ontario, Canada M4V 3B2
(a division of Pearson Penguin Canada Inc.)
Penguin Ireland, 25 St Stephen's Green, Dublin 2, Ireland (a division of Penguin Books Ltd)
Penguin Group (Australia), 250 Camberwell Road,
Camberwell, Victoria 3124, Australia (a division of Pearson Australia Group Pty Ltd)
Penguin Books India Pvt Ltd, 11 Community Centre,
Panchsheel Park, New Delhi – 110 017, India
Penguin Group (NZ), cnr Airborne and Rosedale Roads,
Albany, Auckland 1310, New Zealand (a division of Pearson New Zealand Ltd)
Penguin Books (South Africa) (Pty) Ltd, 24 Sturdee Avenue,
Rosebank, Johannesburg 2196, South Africa

Penguin Books Ltd, Registered Offices: 80 Strand, London WC2R ORL, England

www.penguin.com

My Secret Unicorn: Flying High first published 2002
My Secret Unicorn: Starlight Surprise first published 2003
First published in one volume 2005

2

Text copyright © Working Partners Ltd, 2002, 2003, 2005
Illustrations copyright © Biz Hull, 2002, 2003, 2005
Created by Working Partners Ltd, London W6 0QT
All rights reserved

The moral right of the author and illustrator has been asserted

Set in 25/21.5pt Bembo
Made and printed in England by Clays Ltd, St Ives plc

British Library Cataloguing in Publication Data
A CIP catalogue record for this book is available from the British Library

ISBN 0–141–32003–6

My Secret Unicorn

Flying High

'I wonder what Jessica's doing now,'
she said. 'I wish I knew.'
'Me too,' Twilight said. As he spoke, his
horn touched one of the pink rocks.
There was a bright purple flash.
Twilight shot backwards with a startled
whinny as mist suddenly started to
swirl over the rock.
Lauren leapt to her feet. 'Twilight!'
she gasped.

*To Suzy Higgins — you would
be a wonderful unicorn friend*

CHAPTER

One

Lauren Foster sat at the desk in her bedroom and sighed. The sun was just disappearing behind the Blue Ridge Mountains and the pale sky was streaked with pink and gold. In the paddock behind the house, her pony, Twilight, lifted his head and looked up. How she wished she could be with him, but she had work to do. When Mr Noland, her teacher, had told the class that they were going to do a project on the local mountain range it had sounded like fun. Particularly when he had said that they could work with their friends. However, now that she was faced with drawing a map of all the mountains, streams and valleys, Lauren was rapidly going off the whole project.

She pushed her long, fair hair back behind her ears and wondered how her friends Mel and Jessica were getting on. Jessica was supposed to be drawing pictures of all the animals that lived in the mountains and Mel was going to write about the trees and plants that grew there. Lauren chewed her pencil and

looked at the blank piece of paper in
front of her. She had definitely got the
worst deal!

It wasn't even as if she could ask her
mum and dad for help. Her mum was
working in the study and her dad was
out at a meeting on farming. She'd
checked the bookshelves but there didn't

seem to be any books that might help. And she couldn't use the computer because her mum was working on it.

Lauren made up her mind. It was way too nice an evening to be inside. She could finish the map later. Jumping to her feet, she grabbed her jacket and hurried out of the room.

As she passed the bedroom of her younger brother, Max, she could hear a story-tape playing. She walked on down the corridor and put her head around the study door. 'I'm just going out to see Twilight, Mum,' she said.

Alice Foster was typing quickly, her eyes fixed on the computer screen. She was a children's author and at the moment she was in the middle of writing a new story. 'OK, honey,' she answered vaguely, not even looking round.

'Don't stay out too late.'

'I won't,' Lauren replied. With a feeling of relief, she ran down the stairs and out of the back door.

When Twilight saw Lauren coming down the path, he whinnied and trotted over to meet her.

Lauren's face broke into a smile as it always did at the sight of him. 'Hi, boy,' she said.

Twilight stamped one hoof. With his shaggy mane and scruffy dappled coat, he looked just like any other small grey pony. But he wasn't. Lauren's fingers closed around the hair from his mane that she always kept in her pocket and a familiar sense of excitement tingled through her veins. She glanced around. There was no one nearby. It was safe.

Clutching the hair, Lauren began to whisper the words she knew so well.

Twilight Star, Twilight Star,
Twinkling high above so far.
Shining light, shining bright,
Will you grant my wish tonight?
Let my little horse forlorn
Be at last a unicorn!

As Lauren spoke the final word, there

was a bright purple flash that made her shut her eyes. When she opened them again, Twilight was standing in front of her. But he wasn't a grey pony any more – he was a snowy-white unicorn.

'It worked!' Lauren exclaimed in delight. She'd said the spell many times in the past few weeks since she'd discovered Twilight's hidden powers. Even so, she still couldn't help thinking that one day nothing was going to happen.

'What were you expecting?' Twilight said with a toss of his head. His pearly-white horn caught the last rays of the setting sun and his silver mane and tail shone. He blew on her hands. 'I thought you weren't coming to see me this evening. You said you had homework to do.' His lips didn't move but Lauren could hear him clearly in her head.

'I still have got homework to do,' Lauren said. 'I've got to draw this map of the mountains. But it's really hard.' She sighed. 'I don't know what I'm going to do. I told Mel and Jessica that I'd have it done for tomorrow.'

'But that's easy,' Twilight exclaimed. 'I can fly you over the mountains and you can draw them as we go.'

Lauren stared at him. 'Really?'

'Of course,' Twilight said, tossing his mane.

Lauren grinned. 'Oh, Twilight, you're the best. Come on. Let's go!'

★

Five minutes later, Lauren and Twilight
were cantering through the sky. The wind
whipped Lauren's long hair back from
her face, but she didn't feel cold.
Twilight's silver mane swirled around her
and his body was warm. As they swooped
over the mountains, she laughed out
loud. Flying with Twilight was the
greatest feeling ever!

Lauren took a pen and paper out of
her pocket and began to draw everything
she could see. The wind pulled at the
paper and she had to hang on tight to
stop it blowing away. She was grateful for
Twilight's special unicorn magic that
stopped her from falling off.

'OK, I've drawn the river and the

valleys,' she said, straining her eyes
through the gathering darkness. 'Can we
go a bit lower so that I can see the trees?'

'I can do better than that,' Twilight
said. 'Why don't I go low enough for you
to collect some leaves from them?'

'Wow!' Lauren said in delight. 'I could
stick them on to the poster next to Mel's
drawings.'

Twilight cantered down through the
sky and landed on the soft forest floor.
Lauren picked a leaf from every different
type of tree and bush she could find –
pine, poplar, wild cherry, dogwood – as
well as others for which she didn't know
the names.

'This is great!' she said, getting back on

Twilight's back. 'Our project's going to be the best.'

As Twilight trotted forward, Lauren caught sight of two white-tailed deer, standing in the shadows of the trees. They were staring at Twilight in astonishment. Lauren grinned at the surprise on their faces.

'Where to now?' Twilight asked as he kicked with his back legs and plunged upwards. It was getting very dark.

'We'd better go home,' Lauren said reluctantly. That was the problem about riding Twilight when he was a unicorn – it was only really safe at night when they wouldn't be seen by anyone, and that meant that their rides couldn't go on for

too long. Mrs Fontana, the old lady who
had first told Lauren that unicorns
existed, had warned her that she must
never let Twilight's secret be discovered
by anyone in case it put him in danger.

'Here we go,' Twilight said, jumping
over a treetop as he cantered upwards.
'Hang on!'

Back at Granger's Farm, Twilight landed
safely in his paddock.

'Thank you!' Lauren told him, giving
him a hug.

'You're welcome,' Twilight said,
nuzzling her. 'It was fun.'

Lauren said the words of the Undoing
Spell. There was a purple flash and

suddenly Twilight was a pony again.

'Goodnight, boy,' Lauren whispered, patting him on the neck. And then she ran into the house.

To her relief, her dad wasn't back and her mum was still working. Lauren crept up the stairs and hurriedly got changed into her pyjamas. She glanced at her bedroom clock. It was nine o'clock but she didn't feel tired. That was one of the things she'd found out about flying with Twilight – she never felt tired when she got back. *Maybe it's one of his magical powers*, she thought, as she pulled the roughly drawn map out of her pocket and began to copy it on to a larger piece of paper.

As she worked, she thought about Twilight's magical powers. Mrs Fontana had told her that it was up to every unicorn to discover them for himself. Lauren and Twilight had already found out that he was able to make others feel brave when he touched them with his horn. But it was exciting to think that he might have other powers that they still hadn't discovered.

I wonder what they are, Lauren thought, as she finished drawing the last few mountains on the map. Then she heard her mum's study door open. She threw down her pencil, turned off her light and jumped into bed.

CHAPTER
Two

'This is totally brilliant!' Mel exclaimed as she looked at Lauren's map the next morning.

Lauren grinned happily. She'd got up early to finish the map off and, although it wasn't completely coloured in yet, she had to admit that it looked good. As well as the streams and valleys, she'd drawn all the different sorts of trees and plants she'd seen. 'I've got these as well,' she said, taking the leaves out of her school bag. 'I thought we could stick them on to the edges.'

'Wow!' Mel said, her brown eyes widening. 'Where did you get those from?'

'Oh . . . just around,' Lauren said vaguely. She changed the subject quickly. 'What do you think, Jessica?' she asked, looking at their other friend.

Jessica's head was lowered. She was biting her fingernails and didn't seem to hear Lauren's question.

Mel waved the map under her nose. 'Hey, Jessica. What do you think of Lauren's map?'

'Yeah, yeah – it's great,' Jessica said, not

really looking at it.

Lauren frowned. 'Are you OK?' she asked.

'I'm fine!' Jessica snapped.

Lauren and Mel exchanged surprised glances. It wasn't like Jessica to be cross.

Lauren sat down beside her. 'Want to tell us about it?' she asked in concern.

Jessica's shoulders sagged. 'I'm sorry. It's just . . . well, things aren't very good at home right now.'

'What's wrong?' Mel asked, sitting down on the other side of her.

'Sally's coming to stay for the weekend,' Jessica replied.

'But I thought you liked Sally,' Lauren said.

Jessica's mum
had died when she was little
and Sally was her dad's fiancée. They were
getting married in two weeks' time.

Jessica sighed. 'I do like her. But she's
also bringing Samantha, her daughter.
Samantha normally stays with her dad
when Sally comes to stay, but she'll be
living with us after the wedding. So Sally

thought she should come and stay this weekend.' Jessica swallowed. 'I'm dreading it. I know Samantha doesn't like me.'

Lauren took Jessica's hand and squeezed it. 'I'm sure she does, Jessica. It won't be that bad.'

Jessica looked down at the desk again. She didn't seem convinced.

Nothing seemed to cheer Jessica up that afternoon, not even Mr Noland telling them that their poster was great.

At the end of the day, Lauren, Mel and Jessica walked to the school gates together.

'Mum, Dad and I are flying to Florida tonight,' Mel said. 'We always go to see

my auntie and uncle every Memorial
Day weekend.'

'What about Shadow?' Lauren asked,
thinking about Mel's pony. 'Who's
looking after him?'

'Brad,' said Mel. Brad was one of the
hands who worked on her parents' farm.
'I'll miss Shadow loads, but it'll be fun
being away. Mum said we might even go
to Disneyworld! So I'll see you when I'm
back,' Mel finished, waving as she walked
over to join her parents at the gates.

'Wow!' Lauren said. She turned to see
Jessica's reaction, but Jessica hadn't heard.
She was staring straight ahead. Lauren
followed her gaze. Jessica's dad was
standing with Sally by the school gates

and with them was a slim girl who
looked about eleven. She had sleek, dark-
brown hair and a sulky expression on her
face.

For a moment, Lauren almost thought
that Jessica was going to turn round and
run back into the classroom. But just
then Mr Parker stepped forward.

'Jessica!' he called. 'Over here!'

Jessica had no choice but to go over.
Lauren followed her.

'Hi, girls,' Sally said to them. 'Have you
had a good day?'

'Yes, thanks,' Lauren said.

Jessica just nodded.

Lauren looked at Samantha. The older
girl was scuffing one of her trainers across

the ground. Her brown hair hid her face
and it was impossible to guess what she
was thinking. She didn't look at Jessica
once.

'Well,' Mr Parker said, after a pause, 'I
guess we should be getting home.'

'Dad,' Jessica said suddenly, 'can Lauren
come round at the weekend?'

Lauren looked at her in surprise.

'I don't know, Jess,' Mr Parker began,
looking a bit awkward. 'Another time
might be better. We have got Samantha
staying . . .'

Samantha kicked a stone. 'I don't care
if she has a friend to visit.'

'Samantha!' Sally said, and for a
moment Lauren thought she was going

to tell Samantha off. But then Sally's face softened. 'Please don't use that tone of voice,' she said mildly.

Samantha shrugged and kicked the ground again.

'Please, Dad,' Jessica begged.

Her dad looked at Samantha, then sighed. 'OK.' He turned to Lauren. 'You're very welcome to come round tomorrow morning, Lauren – if it's all right with your mum and dad. Now, we'd better go. Come on, Jessica – the car's round the corner.'

As Lauren watched Jessica and her family walk out of sight, she felt a little sad. She wouldn't want to be Jessica this weekend.

★

As soon as Lauren got home from school, she got changed and went outside to catch Twilight. As she groomed him, she told him about Jessica. He couldn't speak to her when he wasn't a unicorn, but she knew he could understand.

'Jessica's so unhappy,' Lauren told him, as she swept the brush over his neck.

Twilight whickered sympathetically.

'I'm going round there tomorrow morning. I just wish there was something I could do to cheer her up,' Lauren said.

Twilight pushed her with his nose. Lauren frowned. She had a feeling he was trying to tell her something. Twilight nudged at his saddle hanging on the fence. Lauren's eyes widened. Of course!

'I can bring Jessica back here tomorrow and she can ride you!' she exclaimed. 'She loves horses. It's bound to cheer her up.'

Twilight nodded as if that was exactly what he'd been trying to say.

CHAPTER

Three

'Hi, Lauren,' Mr Parker said when Lauren arrived at Jessica's house the next morning. 'Jessica's in the kitchen with Sally and Samantha.'

Lauren went through into the large kitchen. Jessica was sitting at the table, drawing a picture of a horse. Samantha was listening to a Walkman. Her eyes were closed.

'Lauren!' Jessica said, jumping up.

Sally was unloading the dishwasher.
'Hi, Lauren. How are you?'

'Fine thanks,' Lauren replied. She
looked at Jessica's drawing. 'I like your
horse.'

'Thanks,' Jessica said, smiling.

'My little artist,' Mr Parker said fondly
as he came to look at her picture.

Jessica shot an embarrassed look at
Lauren. 'Come on, let's go to my
room.'

'Do you want to take some milk and
cookies with you?' Sally asked.

Lauren and Jessica both nodded eagerly
and while Sally poured two glasses of
milk for them, Jessica fetched the cookie

tin. 'Do you want one, Samantha?' she offered.

But Samantha continued to listen to her Walkman, her eyes closed.

Sally removed the headphones from Samantha's ears.

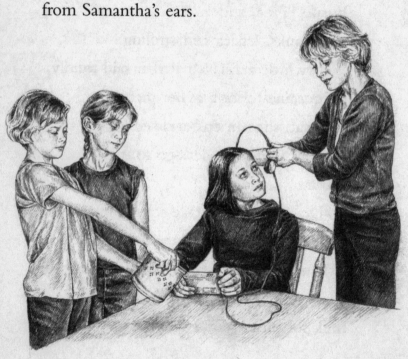

'Mum!' Samantha protested.

'Jessica just asked you if you would like a cookie,' Sally said.

Samantha looked in the tin that Jessica was holding out. 'I don't like any of them,' she said rudely.

Lauren stared. If she'd spoken like that, her mum would have been furious with her, but Sally didn't say anything.

'What sort of cookies do you like then, Samantha?' Mr Parker asked.

Samantha shrugged. 'Pecan and chocolate chip.'

'Well, in that case we should get some when we're out this afternoon,' he said.

'Come on,' Jessica muttered to Lauren. 'Let's go to my room.'

When they reached Jessica's bedroom, Jessica flung herself down on her bed. 'I can't believe how Dad and Sally treat Samantha. She gets her own way about everything. Like this afternoon, Dad's suggested we all go for a game of miniature golf or ten-pin bowling, but no, Samantha doesn't want to do that so we have to spend the afternoon going around the mall instead.' Jessica pulled her knees up to her chest. 'We always do what she wants to do. What's it going to be like after the wedding when she lives here all the time?'

Lauren wanted to comfort her, but she couldn't think of anything to say.

Jessica sniffed and angrily brushed a

tear away from her eyes. 'I'm sorry,' she said.

'It's OK,' Lauren replied. She remembered her plan from the day before. 'Look, why don't we go round to my house and ride Twilight?'

Jessica's eyes lit up. 'Yeah – OK!'

They quickly drank their milk, ate their cookies and took their empty glasses downstairs.

Sally and Samantha were still in the kitchen. Sally was holding Samantha's hands. She broke off as Lauren and Jessica walked in. 'Oh . . . hi, girls.'

Samantha didn't say anything.

Jessica ignored her. 'May Lauren and I go and see Twilight?' she asked Sally.

Sally smiled. 'Sure,' she said. Then she glanced at Samantha. 'Samantha, why don't you go with them? You'd like to see Lauren's pony, wouldn't you?'

Lauren stared at Sally in surprise. This hadn't been part of the plan at all. Anyway, surely Samantha would refuse?

Samantha shrugged. 'I guess I *could* go,' she said.

'I'm sure you'll all have a great time together,' Sally said, beaming happily.

Samantha stood up and looked at Lauren and Jessica. 'Come on, then,' she said abruptly. And with that, she walked out of the kitchen.

Shooting looks of dismay at each other, Lauren and Jessica followed

Samantha outside.

'Where's your house, then?' Samantha said to Lauren.

'About ten minutes away,' Lauren replied. 'It's called Granger's Farm.'

'Right.' Samantha put her headphones on and walked off down the road ahead of them.

'I don't want her to come!' Jessica said to Lauren.

Lauren shook her head, looking at Samantha striding on ahead, and whispered, 'But what can we do?'

CHAPTER

Four

Samantha was waiting for them outside the entrance to Granger's Farm.

'Twilight's down there,' Lauren said, pointing to the path that led round the side of the farmhouse to the paddock.

Samantha shrugged as if she wasn't interested, but followed Lauren and Jessica down the path.

Twilight was standing by the paddock
gate. He whinnied as he saw them.

'Oh, he's lovely!' The words burst out
of Samantha.

Both Lauren and Jessica turned to
stare. Samantha's face had lit up.

'Do you like horses, then?' Jessica asked
her.

But the delight was already leaving
Samantha's face. She shrugged. 'They're
OK,' she said coldly. Then she walked over
to the fence and began to kick at a stone.

Lauren decided to ignore her. She
fetched Twilight's halter and grooming
kit. She and Jessica groomed Twilight
together while Samantha leaned against
the fence.

However, when Lauren and Jessica
went up to the tack room to fetch
Twilight's saddle and bridle, Lauren saw
Samantha go over to Twilight and stroke
his neck.

Twilight behaved perfectly for Jessica.
He cantered round the paddock and then

★ Flying High ★

jumped over a small fence that Lauren's
dad had made.

'Wow!' Jessica said, as she trotted him
back to the gate. 'Twilight's great, Lauren.
He felt like he was flying when he
jumped!'

Twilight gave Lauren a cheeky look
from underneath his long forelock.

Jessica dismounted. 'Are you going to
have a go now, Lauren?'

Lauren nodded, but as she reached to
take Twilight's reins, he stepped forward
and snorted in Samantha's direction.

Lauren guessed what he was trying to
say. 'Samantha, would you like a ride?' she
said.

'Me?' Samantha looked very surprised.

For a moment, Lauren thought she was going to say yes, but then she seemed to think better of it. 'No, no, I won't,' she said abruptly and, crossing her arms, she turned away.

Lauren frowned. She had a feeling Samantha liked horses. But why was she being so unfriendly? She shrugged and glanced at Twilight. He seemed to have a puzzled look on his face too.

Samantha hardly said another word for the rest of the morning. She ignored Lauren and Jessica as they untacked Twilight and brushed him over. 'We should go, Jessica,' she said at last. 'It's almost lunchtime.'

Jessica nodded reluctantly.

As Samantha strode back up the path, Jessica turned to Lauren. 'I wish you were coming with us,' she said. 'The rest of the weekend's going to be awful.'

'It might not be that bad,' Lauren said, trying to cheer her friend up. 'Maybe Samantha will stop being so moody.'

Jessica didn't look convinced.

'Come on, Jessica,' Samantha called irritably from halfway up the drive.

'Bye, Lauren,' Jessica whispered, suddenly sounding as if she was fighting back tears. She gave Twilight a last pat. 'I'd better go.'

Lauren watched her run up the path after Samantha. 'Oh, Twilight,' she said quietly, stroking him. 'I wish we could help.'

That evening, Lauren turned Twilight into a unicorn. 'If only there was something we could do to make Samantha and Jessica get on better,' she said. 'Samantha's so horrid.'

'You know, Samantha was stroking me when you and Jessica weren't there,' Twilight said. 'She was different then. I got the feeling that she was a little sad.'

'But why should she be sad?' Lauren said. 'I mean, I know her mum's getting married again, but Jessica and her dad are really nice.' She frowned. 'And even if she is sad, she shouldn't be so mean to Jessica.

'I know,' Twilight said. 'But it must be hard for Samantha having to move house and adjust to life with a new father and stepsister.'

'I guess,' Lauren reluctantly agreed.

'I think that Samantha's just putting on an act,' Twilight continued. 'I don't think she's really mean. People do strange things when they're unhappy.'

'Well, I wish Samantha would stop it,' Lauren said. 'Jessica's so miserable.'

Twilight nuzzled her. 'Look, why don't we go flying?'

Lauren sighed. 'OK,' she agreed. Maybe that would take her mind off Jessica's problems for a while. 'Let's go to the clearing.'

'OK,' Twilight agreed eagerly.

Lauren climbed on to his back and he cantered upwards into the night sky.

A few minutes later, Twilight flew down between the trees that covered the mountain behind Granger's Farm. He landed lightly on springy grass.

'Wow!' Lauren gasped.

She had never been to the clearing at night before. She had expected it to be dark but it was lit by hundreds of fireflies. They circled and swooped, like tiny moving stars. Lauren slid off Twilight's warm back and breathed in the night air. It was sweet with the heavy scent of the purple flowers that dotted the grass. They were star-shaped and at the tip of each petal a golden spot glowed.

Moonflowers, Lauren thought to herself. She had needed a moonflower when she had first said the spell to turn Twilight into a unicorn. Leaving Twilight, she crouched down and looked at them.

With a soft snort, Twilight moved to the grassy mound at the centre of the clearing. Lowering his head, he began to graze, his long horn touching the grass.

Lauren walked over to him and, for the first time, she noticed that there were some rocks around the base of the mound. In the light from the fireflies they seemed to twinkle and shine with a pink glow. 'Are these magic rocks?' she asked Twilight.

'I don't think so,' Twilight replied. 'They're just made of rose quartz. You find them all through this forest.'

'Oh.' Lauren couldn't help feeling slightly disappointed. She sat down on the grassy mound and watched the fireflies dancing. 'I wonder what Jessica's doing now,' she said. 'I wish I knew.'

'Me too,' said Twilight. As he spoke, his

horn touched one of the pink rocks.
There was a bright purple flash. Twilight
shot backwards with a startled whinny as
mist suddenly started to swirl over the
rock.

Lauren leapt to her feet. 'Twilight!' she
gasped.

Five

Lauren and Twilight stared at the mist
in astonishment.

'What's happening?' Lauren asked,
clutching Twilight's mane.

'I don't know,' Twilight quickly replied.
The mist started fading into the air.

'Look!' Lauren exclaimed. The surface
of the rock was shining like a mirror. It
had a picture in it. Lauren edged closer.

'There are four people,' she gasped. 'A man, a woman and . . .' She broke off and stared. 'Twilight! It's Jessica's house!'

Twilight moved quickly beside her and together they gazed in astonishment at the image on the rock's surface. It was a picture of the main room at Jessica's house. Mr Parker and Sally were sitting on the sofa talking to Samantha. Jessica was sitting by herself on the floor.

Lauren could hear a low buzzing noise. It sounded like voices coming from far, far away. She leaned nearer to the rock. It was voices! Now she was closer to the picture she could hear what everyone was saying . . .

Sally was speaking to Samantha: 'What

would you like to do tomorrow, darling?'

Lauren saw Samantha shrug. 'Go to the mall,' she replied.

'Oh, not again!' Jessica said.

Lauren saw Sally and Mr Parker exchange anxious looks. 'Maybe we could do something else, Sam,' said Mr Parker.

Samantha's face set in a mutinous line. 'There's nothing else worth doing in this stupid town!' she exclaimed.

Lauren looked round at Twilight. 'This is amazing!' she whispered. 'We're watching what's going on in Jessica's house right now. This rock must be magic after all.'

'Maybe it's not the rock,' Twilight said thoughtfully. 'You said you wished you knew what was going on at Jessica's house and I touched the rock with my horn . . .'

'So maybe it's your horn that's working the magic,' Lauren guessed.

Twilight nodded thoughtfully. 'When I was a foal, my mother used to tell me about the wise Golden Unicorns who rule Arcadia,' he said.

'That's the land where all the magic creatures live, isn't it?' Lauren asked, remembering that she had read about Arcadia in the unicorn book she owned.

'Yes,' Twilight replied. 'My mother told me that there are seven Golden Unicorns. They watch over the mortal world using a stone table that shines like a mirror when they touch it with their horns.'

'So, you mean this could be one of

your magical powers?' Lauren asked.

Twilight nodded again. 'Maybe I can see what's going on in other places if I touch a rock with my horn and say what I wish to see.'

'Any rock?' Lauren said excitedly.

'I don't know,' Twilight replied. 'But I guess there's one way to find out.' He trotted to the edge of the clearing where there was a boulder of plain grey granite. 'What shall we try to see?'

'My house,' Lauren suggested.

'I wish I could see Lauren's house,' Twilight said, touching his horn to the stone.

Nothing happened.

'Maybe it's just when you touch a rock

made out of rose quartz, then,' Lauren
said.

Twilight cantered to one of the other
pinky-grey rocks and touched his horn to
it. 'I wish I could see Lauren's house,' he
said.

There was a purple flash and mist
started swirling over the rock.

'It's worked!' Lauren gasped. She ran
over. As the mist cleared, she saw that the
rock's surface was shining. An image of
the outside of her house was slowly
forming, blurry at first but getting
sharper by the second. 'Wow!' she
whispered. She could see her dad's car,
the path to Twilight's paddock and
Buddy, Max's Bernese mountain dog

puppy, sniffing round outside Twilight's
stable.

Twilight touched his horn to the rock
again and, with a slight popping noise,
the picture disappeared.

Lauren went back to the first rock. The picture of Jessica's house was as clear as if she were watching it on television. Jessica was standing up now, looking very upset.

'I don't want to go shopping again tomorrow!' she said.

Her dad sighed. 'Well, we're going to. It's what Samantha wants to do.'

Jessica glared at him. 'Why do we always have to do what she wants, Dad?' she exclaimed, shooting an angry look at Samantha who was sitting on the sofa ignoring her. 'It's not fair!'

'That's enough, Jessica!' Mr Parker spoke firmly.

Lauren saw Jessica bite back a reply and run from the room.

Mr Parker ran a hand through his hair. 'I'd better go and talk to her,' he said.

Lauren turned to Twilight. 'Oh, I wish we could help her. Can't you do anything?'

'But what?' Twilight answered.

'I don't know,' Lauren admitted. She thought hard. 'Maybe Mrs Fontana will help us think of something.'

Mrs Fontana owned a bookshop and knew all about Twilight's unicorn magic.

Twilight nodded eagerly. 'Good idea!'

Lauren glanced at the rock again. Sally had her arm round Samantha and was talking to her. Lauren started to lean forward to listen to what Sally was saying and then changed her mind. It somehow seemed wrong to listen in on a private conversation.

'Please make it go away, Twilight,' she said.

He touched the picture with his horn and it disappeared. Despite the light from the dancing fireflies, the clearing suddenly seemed much darker.

'Come on,' Lauren said, taking hold of Twilight's mane and scrambling on to his back. 'We ought to go home.'

CHAPTER

Six

The next morning, Lauren pushed open the old-fashioned door that led into Mrs Fontana's bookshop. A chime jangled and Walter, Mrs Fontana's black and white terrier, trotted over to meet her, his tail wagging. As Lauren patted him, Mrs Fontana appeared from the back of the shop.

'Hello, Lauren, this is a nice surprise,'

she said, coming over, a smile crinkling up her lined face. As always, her long grey hair was pinned up in a bun and she had a mustard-yellow shawl around her shoulders. 'So, what can I do for you?'

Lauren glanced round, wondering whether it was safe to talk.

'It's OK,' Mrs Fontana said. 'You're the only person here.' Her bright blue eyes searched Lauren's face. 'I take it this visit is about Twilight?'

Lauren nodded.

'Why don't we sit down?' Mrs Fontana said, waving to one of the armchairs that nestled among the piles of books – new and second-hand – that rose from the

floor like wobbly towers. 'So, tell me,'
Mrs Fontana said, sitting opposite her.
'What's the problem?'

Lauren explained about Jessica and
then about the night before in the
clearing. As she explained how Twilight's
horn made the picture appear in the rose
quartz rock, Mrs Fontana chuckled.

'That must have given you a shock,' she
said.

'Yes, it did,' Lauren said, grinning.

'That was always one of my favourite
unicorn powers.' A smile played across the
old lady's face and Lauren had the sudden
feeling that Mrs Fontana was reliving old
memories. With a blink, Mrs Fontana
seemed to come back to the present. 'So,
what is it you want to know?'

'Can Twilight help my friend?' Lauren
said.

'Of course he can!' Mrs Fontana smiled. 'But I can't tell you how. You and Twilight must learn how to use his powers for yourself. With your good heart and his courage, I know you'll find a way.'

Lauren felt disappointed. 'But I've been thinking and thinking what we can do,' she said, 'and I still don't know. Is there anything you can suggest?'

Mrs Fontana's voice dropped and she leaned forward. 'It might help you to know that there is a way that someone else can see Twilight. If a person drinks the Unseeing Potion, it will make them forget they have ever seen a unicorn. However,' her eyes seemed to bore into

Lauren, 'the Unseeing Potion will only work if it is taken knowingly and willingly. You can only reveal Twilight's secret to someone you can trust to drink the potion. If you reveal his secret to the wrong person, then his life could be put in danger.'

Lauren's thoughts were spinning – a potion that meant someone else could see Twilight safely. That was amazing! A thought struck her. 'But I don't see how this helps Jessica,' she said.

Mrs Fontana smiled. 'As I said, how you use Twilight's powers is up to you.' She seemed to see the frustration on Lauren's face. 'Oh, my dear, please believe me, I am not trying to make your life difficul...

is a reas...

Twilight...

use them...

'But w...

Mrs Fo...

day, you w...

Just then ...alter gave a sharp bark. Mrs
Fontana glanced at the door. 'There is
someone coming,' she said quickly. 'We
cannot talk any more now. Use the
advice I have given you wisely, my dear.
Promise me you will take great care
before you reveal Twilight's secret to
anyone.'

'I will,' Lauren promised.

The shop door opened and Mrs Foster

looked in, holdi...
bags. 'Hello...
smiling...
sai...

ng armfuls of shopping

, Mrs Fontana,' she said,

. 'Ah, there you are, Lauren,' she

, catching sight of Lauren sitting in

the chair. 'I've bought the things I needed

from town. Are you ready to go?'

Lauren nodded and got to her feet.
'Bye, Mrs Fontana.'

'Goodbye, Lauren,' Mrs Fontana
replied. Her eyes twinkled. 'No doubt I'll
see you again soon.'

As Lauren reached the door, Mrs
Fontana came after her. 'Oh, Lauren. You
might need this.' She pressed a folded
piece of paper into Lauren's hand.

'Thanks,' Lauren said, wondering what
the note was.

Lauren read the first few words as they walked to the car: *Take two moonflowers and a hair from a unicorn's mane . . .*

It was the Unseeing Potion!

'What's that, honey?' her mum asked.

Lauren quickly folded the paper up and put it in her pocket. 'Oh nothing,' she said quickly. 'Nothing important.'

CHAPTER
Seven

'I'm going to take Twilight out for a ride,' Lauren said to her mum when they got back home.

It only took her ten minutes to give Twilight a quick brush over and tack him up. 'Just wait till you hear what I've got to tell you,' she said, as she pulled down the stirrups and mounted. 'Come on – we're going to the clearing.'

Sensing her excitement, Twilight pulled at the bit. As soon as they had trotted out of the farm and on to the track that led into the wood, Lauren leaned forward and let Twilight canter. His hooves thudded along the sandy track until they reached the hidden path that led to the clearing.

At the end of the path, the trees parted and Twilight trotted into the open space. Shafts of sunlight shone down through the leafy canopy and lit up the grass. Pink and yellow butterflies fluttered through the air. Lauren stopped Twilight and slid off. 'I'm going to turn you into a unicorn,' she told him, as she started to untack him. 'I know it's daytime but no one can see us here and we need to talk.'

Twilight nodded his head and snorted as if he agreed.

'OK,' said Lauren, sliding the saddle off his back and putting it on the grass. 'Here goes.'

A few moments later, Twilight was a unicorn. It felt strange for Lauren. Until now, she'd only ever said the spell in the evening. It didn't seem right to have the sun shining down on his snowy-white coat and silvery horn. But Twilight didn't seem to find anything odd about it at all.

'So what did Mrs Fontana say?' he asked.

'She gave me this,' Lauren replied,

getting the piece of paper out of her
pocket. She read out what Mrs Fontana
had written:

Take two moonflowers and a
hair from a unicorn's mane
and put them in water under
the light of the moon. After
ten seconds, the flowers and
the hair will have dissolved in
the water and the potion will
be ready to drink. Within
thirty seconds, the person who
has drunk it will have
forgotten they have ever seen
a unicorn.

'So if someone drinks the potion they won't remember having seen me?' Twilight said.

'That's right,' Lauren told him.

'But what would happen if the person changed their mind and decided not to drink the potion?' Twilight said.

'Mrs Fontana said that was a risk,' Lauren replied. 'She told me that we have to be very careful about whom we choose to reveal your secret to.'

'But I don't understand how it would help Jessica to be able to see me,' said Twilight.

Lauren sighed. 'Neither do I. But I'm sure Mrs Fontana wouldn't have given us the recipe unless it could help. I guess

we've just got to think about it a bit
longer.' She glanced round. Although the
glade was the most secret place she could

think of, there was still a chance that
someone might come along. 'We'd better
turn back now. I'll come and visit you
tonight and we'll see if we can think of a
plan then.'

'OK,' Twilight agreed.

Lauren kissed his nose and then said
the words of the Undoing Spell. There
was a purple flash and Twilight was a
pony once more.

As Lauren rode back along the main
forest track, she glanced at her watch. She
might as well ride Twilight for a little bit
longer.

'Let's go to Jessica's,' she said to
Twilight. 'We won't stop for long but it

might cheer her up to see us.'

Twilight nodded and they trotted along the road to Jessica's house.

Sally was watering the pots of flowers at the front of the house. 'Hello, Lauren,' she said, smiling as Lauren turned Twilight into the driveway. 'Have you come to see Jessica?'

'Yes,' Lauren said, thinking how nice she was. 'I just thought I'd say hi.'

'I'll go and get her,' Sally said. 'And maybe your pony would like some water? I could fetch a bucket from the back yard.'

'That would be great,' Lauren said, smiling at her and dismounting.

Sally went into the house. A minute

later, Jessica came running out of the front door. 'Lauren! Sally said you were here! Oh, Twilight,' she said, giving him a hug. He nuzzled her, leaving a messy mark on her T-shirt. Jessica grinned, not seeming to mind a bit.

'It's really good to see you,' she said to Lauren.

'How's it going?' Lauren asked her anxiously. Although Jessica was smiling now, her eyes looked suspiciously red, as if she'd recently been crying.

'Oh, it's not too bad,' Jessica said. She spoke bravely, but Lauren could tell she was upset. 'I've got to go and try a bridesmaid's dress on this afternoon,' Jessica continued. She swallowed, then burst out, 'Oh, Lauren, I just don't want the wedding to happen! Samantha was so mean last night.'

Lauren only just stopped herself from saying 'I know'.

'Er . . . how?' she asked.

'Oh, the usual,' Jessica said. 'I got a bit mad and Dad came to talk to me. He said I've got to try and be more understanding. He said that he knows Samantha seems difficult to get on with but it's just because she's upset about leaving her school and friends to come and live here. But I think it's because she just doesn't like me!'

'Of course she does,' Lauren started to say. 'Maybe your dad has a point –'

'But she *doesn't* like me, Lauren!' Jessica interrupted, her blue eyes welling with tears. 'And I don't want to have to live with her!'

Just then the back gate opened and Sally came out with a bucket of water and a couple of carrots. 'Here we are,' she said cheerfully. 'I thought he might be hungry as well.'

'Thanks,' Lauren said, glancing at Jessica, who had hidden her face from Sally by stroking Twilight's neck.

'Well,' Sally said, putting down the bucket. 'I'll leave you two to it, then. Don't stay out here too long, Jessica. Remember we've got the bridesmaid's dress fitting this afternoon.'

Jessica nodded.

As Sally went inside, Lauren looked anxiously at Jessica. 'Are you OK?'

Jessica sniffed. 'I guess I'll have to be,' she said in a small voice. 'See you, Lauren.'

How I wish this wedding wasn't
happening!'

Lauren sighed. If only she could think
of some way of helping . . .

The minutes seemed to crawl by so
slowly until the evening. Lauren was
longing to be able to go and talk things
over with Twilight. As soon as she and
Max had finished filling the dishwasher
with their dirty plates, Lauren put her
trainers on. 'I'm just going to see
Twilight,' she said to her parents.

'OK, honey,' her dad said. He looked
under the kitchen table, where Max was
playing with Buddy. 'Come on, Max.
Time for your bath.'

Just as he and Max were going up the stairs, the phone rang. 'Lauren, can you get that for me, please?' he called.

Lauren jumped to her feet and picked up the receiver. 'Granger's Farm. Who's speaking, please?'

'Lauren. It's Jessica's dad here.' Mr Parker's voice was tense and tight, and in the background Lauren was sure she could hear someone crying.

'Oh, hello,' Lauren started to say, wondering why he was ringing. 'Do you want to speak to my –'

Mr Parker cut her off. 'Lauren, have you seen Jessica in the last couple of hours?'

Lauren frowned. 'No. Why?'

'She's gone missing,' Mr Parker said.
'We think she's run away!'

CHAPTER

Eight

For a moment, Lauren was too shocked to speak. 'Run away!' she stammered at last.

'Can I speak to your father, please?' Mr Parker asked.

'Dad!' Lauren shouted.

Mr Foster came hurrying down the stairs. 'What's the matter?' he asked, seeing her pale face.

'Jessica's run away!' Lauren exclaimed.

Her dad took the phone. Lauren's legs felt shaky and she sat down at the table. It was still light outside at the moment, but soon it would get dark. What would Jessica do then?

'I'll come over and help you look, Jack,' she heard her father saying quickly. 'I'll tell Alice what's happening. She can ring if Jessica turns up here.' There was a pause and then Mr Foster nodded. 'Sure. I'll be with you as soon as I can.'

He put the phone down.

'Can I come with you?' Lauren asked, jumping to her feet.

'I think it's best if you stay here,' Mr Foster said. 'Everyone at the Parkers' is

very upset just now – particularly
Samantha. Mr Parker said she seems to
think it's all her fault.'

Mr Foster saw the worry on his
daughter's face and gave her a quick hug.
'It'll be all right,' he said comfortingly.
'We'll find Jessica. Don't you worry.'

Five minutes later, Lauren was alone in
the kitchen. Her mum and Max were
upstairs and her dad had gone to the
Parkers'. She went to the window and
stared out into the dusk. If only she knew
where Jessica was.

And it was then that an idea struck
her. Of course! Twilight's magic powers
could show her. They only had to look

into the rock. Why hadn't she thought of it before?

She pulled open the door and raced outside.

'Twilight!' she cried, running down the path to the paddock. 'Quick! I need your help.'

Twilight was already standing by the gate. He began to whinny frantically.

'Jessica's gone missing,' she gasped. 'We need to go to the wood and –'

A neigh from Twilight cut across her words. He reared up, his front hooves stamping down on the grass.

'What's the matter?' Lauren asked in astonishment. The only other time she'd ever seen him looking so agitated was when Max and Buddy had almost caught her turning him into a unicorn. Her eyes suddenly widened. Maybe there was someone nearby?

She spun around, half-expecting to see someone, but there were only the familiar shapes of the trees and bushes, shadowy against the night sky.

'What is it?' she asked Twilight.

Twilight stamped his front hoof. Lauren listened. In the silence, she heard a sudden rustle.

Her heart almost jumped out of her chest. The noise had come from a large bush near the gate. Taking a deep breath, she walked forward. 'Hello,' she called, trying to sound brave. 'Is there anyone there?'

Through the silence of the night came the sound of a sob. Lauren ran forward, suddenly no longer afraid. She reached into the bush and pushed the branches aside.

'Jessica!' she gasped.

Jessica was crouching in the hollow centre of the bush. Her face was streaked with tears. When she saw Lauren she buried her head in her hands and sobbed again.

'What are you doing here?' Lauren asked.

Jessica showed no signs of answering and so Lauren pushed her way through the brambles towards her. 'Please come out.' She put an arm around Jessica's shoulders and helped her out of the bush. Twilight came over and nuzzled Jessica's cold hands.

'Everyone's looking for you,' Lauren said, staring at her friend. 'What's wrong?'

'Everything.' Jessica put her arms round Twilight's neck and buried her face in his mane. 'I don't want to go home ever again, Lauren.'

'Why? What's happened?' Lauren asked.

Jessica sniffed. 'This afternoon was awful. We went to try the bridesmaids' dresses on and Samantha refused to have the shoes or headdresses that we had chosen and made out that I'm just a little

kid who doesn't know anything. Then she wouldn't speak to her mum because Sally said that my opinion did matter. Worst of all, when we got home, Dad said he and Sally have decided that when Samantha moves in after the wedding, she's going to share my bedroom.'

'Share your bedroom!' Lauren echoed.

Jessica nodded. 'Dad says that they think it will help us get to know each other better. But I don't want to get to know Samantha,' she wailed. 'She hates me and I bet she's glad I've run away.'

Lauren shook her head. 'She's not — she's really upset.'

'As if,' Jessica said.

'She is,' Lauren insisted. 'Your dad said.'

'It's just an act, then,' Jessica said. 'She doesn't care about me at all.' And with that, she began to cry again.

Lauren hugged her, wishing that she could show Jessica that Samantha did care.

Twilight whinnied. Lauren looked at him. He turned to look in the direction of the wood.

Lauren caught her breath. Of course! There actually was a way that she could show Jessica that Samantha was upset. But it would mean revealing Twilight's secret.

Leaving Jessica for a moment, Lauren went over to Twilight. 'Are you sure?' she whispered into his ear.

Twilight whickered softly and nodded his head.

'OK,' Lauren told him. She turned to her friend. 'Jessica, I'm sure I can prove that Samantha really does care about you.'

Jessica frowned. 'How?'

'I'll tell you in a second,' Lauren said. 'But first you have to promise that afterwards you'll do whatever I ask.'

'All right,' Jessica said. 'I promise.'

Lauren swallowed. 'OK.' She took Jessica's hand. 'Look, don't be shocked, but Twilight isn't just a pony, Jessica. He's . . . well . . .' she took a deep breath, 'he's a unicorn.'

For a moment, Jessica looked at her in stunned silence and then, despite her unhappiness, she laughed. 'A unicorn!' she said. 'Don't be silly, Lauren!'

'No, he is,' Lauren said.

Jessica stared at her. 'Unicorns don't exist. They're just make-believe –'

'Just watch,' Lauren interrupted. She swung round and quickly said the magic spell and suddenly Twilight was standing there – a unicorn once more.

Lauren thought Jessica was going to faint.

'But . . . but . . .' Jessica stammered, staring at him, her eyes wide.

'See, unicorns do exist,' Lauren said.

Jessica walked slowly to Twilight. 'He's so beautiful!' With a shaking hand she reached out and touched his neck. 'Oh, wow!' she breathed. 'Just wait till everyone hears about this!'

'You can't tell anyone, Jessica,' Lauren said quickly. 'It has to be a secret.'

Jessica frowned. 'But I don't understand,' she said.

'We'll talk about it later,' Lauren said. Time was passing and with every minute that went by she knew that Jessica's family would be feeling more and more worried. First she had to carry out her plan, then she and Twilight had to get Jessica home as quickly as they could. She looked at Twilight. 'Can you carry us both?'

'Yes, of course,' Twilight said.

Jessica almost jumped out of her skin. 'He can talk!' she exclaimed.

'Yes, but you can only hear him if you're touching him or holding a hair from his mane,' Lauren told her. She saw Jessica's mouth start to open with a question. 'Come on, I'll explain on the way.'

As Twilight flew to the clearing in the wood, Lauren told Jessica all about unicorns and how she had discovered Twilight's secret. Jessica was thrilled. 'So there are other unicorns in the world?' she said as Twilight began to fly down through the trees.

'Yes,' Lauren said. 'But they just look like grey ponies. They can only turn into a unicorn if they find someone who believes in magic enough to say the Turning Spell.'

'Like you did,' Jessica said as Twilight

landed on the soft grass.

Lauren nodded and dismounted.

'I'd give anything to have a unicorn of my own,' Jessica said longingly. She slid off Twilight's back and looked around at the fireflies dancing through the dusky air. 'What a cool place,' she breathed. 'But why are we here?'

'We're going to show you how Samantha feels about you being missing,' Lauren said, walking over to one of the pinky-grey rocks. She desperately hoped that her plan was going to work.

Twilight joined her. 'I wish I could see Samantha,' she said, and Twilight touched the stone with his horn.

Jessica gasped as the purple light

flashed and mist started to swirl. She grabbed Lauren's arm.

'It's OK,' Lauren told her. 'Watch what happens now.'

Just as before, the mist slowly cleared to show the surface of the rock beginning to shine like a mirror. As they watched, two shadowy shapes in the mirror gradually became clearer.

'It's Samantha and Sally!' Jessica exclaimed in astonishment.

The mirror showed a picture of the kitchen at Jessica's house. Samantha and her mum were sitting at the table.

'You need to get close to be able to hear what they're saying,' Lauren said to Jessica.

They crouched down together.

'She's been out for hours now, Mum,'
Samantha was sobbing. 'What if she
doesn't come back?'

'She will,' Sally soothed, stroking her hair. 'I'm sure Jack will find her soon.'

'But what if he doesn't? Oh, Mum, it's all my fault,' Samantha cried. 'I was so mean to her. I wish I hadn't been. It's just I've been so scared about coming to live here. It's Jessica's life and Jessica's house and I feel like an outsider.'

'I know, Sam,' her mum said. 'But our house is too far away from Jack's work for us to live there.' She stroked her hair. 'I promise it won't take you long to settle in and make new friends here. And I'm sure Jessica will help you.'

'If she ever comes back,' Samantha said. 'What if something bad has happened to her?' More tears spilled out of her eyes.

'Oh, Mum, I'm so worried about her.'

Sally hugged her tight, but as she lifted her eyes upwards Lauren could see how strained and worried she looked.

Lauren glanced at Jessica. Her face was pale and shocked. Lauren reached out and took her hand. 'See? It won't be that bad when your dad and Sally get married,' she said softly. 'And maybe having a sister will be fun.'

Jessica swallowed hard and looked at Twilight. 'Can you show me what it will be like?' she asked.

Twilight shook his head. 'No one can see into the future, not even unicorns.' He nuzzled her shoulder. 'The future's up to you, Jessica. It's what you make it. But

now you know how Samantha feels, I'm
sure it can all work out – if you want it to.'

Jessica took a deep breath. 'I want it to,'
she said. She glanced at the mirror again.
'There's Dad,' she said suddenly. 'Look!'

Mr Parker had just come into the
picture. Lauren and Jessica both bent
forward to hear what was going on.

Sally had jumped to her feet. 'Have
you found her?'

Mr Parker shook his head. 'I thought
I'd check back here to see if she's called.'

Sally shook her head. 'No . . . no, she
hasn't.'

Mr Parker ran his hand through his
hair. 'Where is she?' he groaned. 'It's this
wedding. I know it is.'

'Perhaps we should call it off,' Sally said, looking worried.

'No!' Jessica exclaimed. She looked at Lauren and Twilight. Her eyes were suddenly glinting with tears. 'Take me home, Twilight,' she said. 'Please!'

CHAPTER

Nine

As Jessica clambered on to Twilight's snowy-white back, Lauren bent down and picked two purple moonflowers from the grass. She felt a flutter of fear. Was Jessica going to keep her promise to do whatever Lauren asked when they dropped her back home?

The flight home was tense. Lauren could sense how anxious Jessica was to let her family know that she was safe. It seemed like forever before Twilight landed gently under the cover of some trees near Jessica's house.

'We need to wait a moment,' Lauren told Jessica as they dismounted.

'But I want to get home as quickly as possible,' Jessica said.

'It'll only take a minute,' Lauren assured her. 'We need to do something.'

'What?' Jessica asked.

Lauren took a deep breath. 'Well, you remember that before I turned Twilight into a unicorn I made you promise that you would do whatever I asked?' she said.

'Yes,' Jessica said.

'Well, you've got to drink a potion that

will make you forget you've ever seen
Twilight. That's what this water is for,' she
said, taking a little bottle out of her
pocket. 'It's to make the potion.'

'I won't remember anything about him
at all?' Jessica said a little sadly.

Lauren shook her head.

'But . . . but . . .' Jessica seemed lost for
words.

'It's to keep him safe,' Lauren said. 'If
anyone else knows about him, he could
be in real danger.'

'I think I understand,' Jessica said slowly.

'So you'll drink the potion?' Lauren
asked her.

Jessica nodded. 'Yes,' she said.

'Well, all I need to do is add the

flowers and a hair of Twilight's mane to this water,' Lauren said. 'And then we put it in the moonlight for ten seconds and it's ready to drink.'

She broke off a single hair from Twilight's mane and dropped it into the bottle with the two flowers. The water immediately fizzed and bubbled and turned purple. Lauren held it up to a shaft of moonlight that was filtering down through the trees. As they watched, the purple faded and the liquid became clear. A sweet smell floated off it, like lemonade.

'It's ready,' Lauren said, after she had counted to ten. She held the bottle out to Jessica.

Jessica stroked the unicorn's neck.
'Goodbye, Twilight,' she said softly.
Twilight blew gently on her face and

then she took the bottle. 'Here goes,' she said, and in one gulp she drained the liquid.

Lauren watched her. She sort of expected something to happen – a purple flash or something – but nothing did.

'Thank you,' Jessica said, handing the bottle back to Lauren. 'It tasted sort of sweet and fruity.' She frowned. 'But it hasn't made me forget about Twilight.'

'The spell said that it takes thirty seconds to work,' Twilight said.

Lauren looked towards the house. 'You'd better go,' she said to Jessica. The curtains hadn't been drawn across the kitchen windows and she could see Mr Parker pacing up and down while Sally

hugged Samantha at the kitchen table.
'Everyone's worried about you. Let them
know you're all right.'

'OK,' Jessica said. 'Bye!' And with that
she began to run across the lawn. But just
as she reached the back door, she
stopped.

'What's she doing?' Lauren whispered
to Twilight as Jessica looked round in a
confused way.

'I think the potion's just worked,' he
said softly.

As they watched, Jessica shook her
head and ran on into the house.

From the shelter of the trees, Twilight
and Lauren watched the kitchen window.
They saw the worry on Mr Parker's face

clear in an instant as Jessica ran into the
room. Sally and Samantha jumped to
their feet in relief. And they saw Jessica
being pulled into a big family hug.

Lauren swallowed the lump of happy
tears in her throat. 'Oh, Twilight, I think
life's going to be better for Jessica from
now on,' she said.

He stamped his hoof. 'I think you're
right,' he replied.

Two weeks later, Lauren rode Twilight up
to Jessica's house. A big white car was
parked in their driveway and, as Lauren
halted Twilight to have a look at it, the
front door of the house opened and
Jessica and Samantha ran out. They were

dressed in cream bridesmaids' dresses and they were smiling.

'They're never going to get there on time,' Lauren heard Samantha say.

'Dad's always late!' Jessica said to Samantha.

'That makes two of them,' Samantha told her.

Jessica laughed. Lauren didn't think she'd ever seen her friend look happier. 'Dad! We're going to be late!' Jessica shouted.

The door opened wider and Sally and Mr Parker appeared. Sally was dressed in a beautiful light blue dress and Mr Parker was wearing a smart grey suit.

'Come on!' Jessica insisted, getting hold

of her dad's arm and dragging him to
the car.

Just then Sally caught sight of Lauren.
'Hi!' she called, waving. 'Jessica –
it's Lauren!'

Jessica came racing over.

'Lauren! Lauren!' she gasped. 'Dad's just told me the best news. He's going to get me and Samantha a pony as a wedding present. It turns out she loves horses just as much as I do!'

'That's brilliant!' Lauren exclaimed.

Mr Parker beeped the car's horn. 'Jessica! You'll make us late!'

Jessica looked indignant. 'Me? Make you late!'

Samantha leaned out of the window. 'Hi, Lauren. Come on, Jessica!'

'I'd better go,' Jessica said to Lauren. She reached to pat Twilight goodbye and suddenly a puzzled look crossed her face. She frowned, almost as if she was trying to remember something. 'You know, I had this really funny dream about Twilight . . .' she began.

The car's horn sounded. Jessica's expression cleared. 'Oh, it doesn't matter,' she said, shaking her head. 'See you in school!' And with that she ran to the car.

As Jessica got in, Lauren waved and Twilight whinnied. Then the car pulled out of the driveway and set off down the road.

Lauren looked at Twilight and smiled. Their secret was safe. Once again, only she knew that her pony was a unicorn in disguise.

My Secret Unicorn

Starlight Surprise

Touching her heels to Twilight's sides,
Lauren rode him down the overgrown path.
As they got nearer, the tree house seemed to
loom up in front of them. Its old grey walls
were covered with green moss and the air
around it seemed still and silent. A shiver ran
down Lauren's spine. It did look kind of
spooky. Her heart started to beat faster. It
couldn't really be haunted, could it?

To my parents, for everything ★

CHAPTER
One

'Faster, Twilight! Faster!' Lauren Foster cried, burying her hands in Twilight's soft mane.

With a whinny, Twilight surged forward. Lauren's light-brown hair blew back behind her and she laughed out loud as Twilight swooped through the night air, the moonlight shining on his silvery horn.

Lauren loved these moments – the secret times when Twilight, her pony, changed into a magical flying unicorn.

'This is fun!' Twilight exclaimed.

'It sure is!' Lauren agreed as the wind whipped her cheeks. Far below, she could see the treetops and farmhouse where she lived with her mum, dad and younger brother, Max. Her family didn't know about Twilight's secret. In fact, right now, they thought she was in the paddock giving Twilight his evening feed. Lauren smiled as she imagined how amazed they would be if they could see her flying through the moonlit sky instead.

Suddenly Twilight pricked up his ears. 'Hey, listen – what's that noise?' he asked.

Lauren heard a frightened bleating
sound.

'It's coming from the woods,' Twilight
decided. 'It sounds like an animal in
trouble.'

'Let's go and see what it is,' Lauren said immediately.

Twilight cantered down among the trees.

As they got lower, Lauren saw a young fawn caught in a thicket of brambles.

'Oh, look!' she cried. 'The poor thing's all tangled up.'

The thorns were caught in the fawn's russet-red coat and a wiry branch had wrapped itself around one of his legs. No matter how the baby deer struggled, he couldn't get free. His mother watched anxiously from nearby. Seeing Twilight landing on the grass, she shied back in panic. The fawn redoubled his efforts to break free, stamping his hooves in terror.

'We *have* to help him,' Lauren said determinedly.

Twilight nodded and approached the fawn. With a quiet whicker, he touched his horn gently against the fawn's neck. In moments, the terror magically ebbed from the deer's eyes. He stopped struggling and stood still.

Lauren dismounted. Ignoring the thorns that grabbed and tore at her bare hands, she crouched down and began to pull the wiry bramble from around the fawn's leg.

'There you are, baby,' she said at last. 'You're free now.'

Twilight lifted his horn from the fawn's neck and used it to sweep aside

the brambles. With a snort, the fawn leapt
out of the thicket and ran to his mother's
side.

The two deer looked at Twilight in
astonishment, then bounded away into
the forest.

'It doesn't matter that they've seen

you, does it?' Lauren asked Twilight as she picked her way out of the brambles.

Twilight shook his head. 'Most animals know that a unicorn's secret must be kept. It's other people who must never be allowed to find out about me in case they try to use my magic for bad things.'

Lauren put her arm over Twilight's neck. There was a warm glow in her heart. 'I'm glad we were here to help.'

'Me too,' Twilight agreed. He nuzzled her hands. 'But you've hurt yourself,' he said with concern.

Lauren looked at the deep scratches on her hands. She shrugged. 'It was worth it.'

Twilight bent his head and his horn gently touched Lauren's scratches.

Warmth seemed to flood over Lauren's
hands and she gasped. The scratches
tingled sharply for a few seconds and
then all of a sudden the pain disappeared.
Lauren stared. Where the wounds had
been, there were just some faint pink
marks. 'Wow!' she said, looking at
Twilight in amazement. 'I didn't know
you could do that!'

'Me neither,' Twilight said, looking equally surprised.

'It must be unicorn magic,' Lauren said.

Twilight nodded. Unicorns had many magical powers but neither he nor Lauren knew what they all were yet. Ever since Lauren had first changed him into a unicorn they had been finding out what his powers were.

Taking hold of his mane, Lauren swung herself up on to his back. 'We should go home. If I'm gone too long, Mum or Dad will come outside to find out what I'm doing. We mustn't risk them seeing you.'

With one push of his powerful hind

legs, Twilight kicked up into the sky and
they headed back to Granger's Farm.

As they landed in Twilight's paddock,
Lauren hugged him. 'I'm going to keep
you forever,' she told him happily as she
dismounted. 'We'll always live here,' she
went on, looking around at the fields and
outbuildings of her parents' new farm,
'and if I ever have kids, they can learn to
ride on you and they'll believe in
unicorns too!' But then a worrying
thought struck her. 'How . . . how long
do unicorns live, Twilight?'

Twilight looked puzzled. 'I'm not sure.'
He snorted. 'I don't really know much
about being a unicorn. I left the land

where I was born when I was a young
foal and I haven't met any other unicorns
since.'

'We must find out,' Lauren told him.

Twilight looked thoughtful. 'I bet Mrs
Fontana would know.'

Lauren nodded. Mrs Fontana was an
old lady who owned a second-hand
bookshop and the only other person who
knew about Twilight. She too had found
a unicorn when she was a young girl.
When Lauren had first got Twilight, Mrs
Fontana had given her a book about
unicorns that had contained the spell she
needed to turn Twilight into his magical
form. 'I'll ask her next time I see her,'
Lauren said.

She looked towards the lights of the farmhouse. They seemed very bright in the darkness. It was getting late. 'I should go in,' she said. Giving Twilight a pat, she said the words that would turn him back into a pony.

'Twilight Star, Twilight Star,
Twinkling high above so far,
Protect this secret from prying eyes
And return my unicorn to his disguise.
His magical shape is for my eyes only,
Let him be once more a pony.'

There was a purple flash and then Twilight was standing there – no longer a unicorn but a rather shaggy thirteen-hand grey pony.

He lifted his muzzle to her face. Lauren kissed his soft nose. 'See you tomorrow, Twilight,' she whispered. Then she turned and hurried to the house.

CHAPTER
Two

When Lauren went down for breakfast the next morning, she found her mum and Max already up. Her brother was sitting on their mother's knee. Lauren stared. Now that Max was six, he almost never sat on their mum's knee.

'Bad dream,' Mrs Foster mouthed to Lauren over Max's curly dark head.

Lauren nodded understandingly and,

patting Buddy, Max's Bernese mountain dog puppy who was sitting beside the table, she sat down.

'Lauren,' Max said slowly, as Lauren poured herself some cereal. 'Do you believe in ghosts?'

'No,' Lauren said, looking at him in surprise. 'Why?'

'Because there's a tree house by the creek that everyone says is haunted,' Max replied.

Mrs Foster frowned. 'Is this what your bad dream was about, Max?'

Max nodded.

'But, honey,' Mrs Foster said, turning him so she could see his face, 'ghosts don't exist.'

'But Matthew and David say they saw one,' Max said. 'It was white and it floated through the air above the tree house *and* it made noises.' He looked scared.

'Oh, Max,' Mrs Foster said. 'It was probably a bird. They just *thought* it was a ghost.'

'Yeah, Mum's right. There are no such things as ghosts, Max,' Lauren said, backing her mum up.

But Max didn't look convinced.

'Do you want to go for a ride in the woods after school, Lauren?' asked Mel, one of Lauren's friends. They were leaving the classroom at morning break.

'Definitely,' Lauren replied.

Jessica, their other friend, sighed longingly. 'I wish I had my pony. Then I could come too,' she said. Jessica's dad had promised to buy her a pony in the summer holidays, but that was still ages away.

'You can still come,' Lauren said, not wanting Jessica to feel left out. 'Bring your bike and we can swap. You can ride Twilight some of the time while I ride your bike.'

Jessica's face lit up. 'That would be great!'

Just then, three boys from another class came running down the corridor. They barged past, bumping into Jessica so that she stumbled and fell over. 'Hey!' Lauren

called angrily as they ran on, laughing,
not even bothering to stop and see if
Jessica was OK.

'Ow!' Jessica said, picking herself up off the floor.

'Idiots!' Lauren said, staring after the boys.

Mel nodded. 'It was Nick, Dan and Andrew – Nick's the tall one, Dan's the one with the freckles and Andrew's got the curly hair. They're in my cousin Katie's class. She says they're really mean.'

'Well, she's obviously right,' Lauren said. She hadn't come across the three boys before. Her family had only moved into Granger's Farm recently, and she didn't know everyone at her new school yet.

The three girls started talking again about the ride they were going to go on that afternoon. 'It's so hot – we could visit the creek,' Mel suggested.

'Yeah,' Jessica agreed. 'Shadow and Twilight can go in the water – they'll like that.'

Lauren thought about Silver Creek, the small river that wound its way down from the mountains, through the woods, and remembered the conversation over breakfast. 'You'll never guess what Max said this morning,' she told them with a grin. 'He said that there's a tree house near the creek that's haunted!'

To her surprise, Mel and Jessica didn't grin back.

'Yeah, we know,' Mel said seriously.

'It's up a little path away from the

creek,' Jessica said. 'It's totally spooky.'

Lauren stared at them. 'It can't be haunted, surely?'

Mel's shoulder-length curls bounced as she nodded quickly. 'Jen and Sarah went near it a while back and they said they saw a ghost in the trees!'

'Really?' Lauren said, her eyes widening, as she remembered that Max's friends had told him the same thing.

'But there are loads of other trails that lead to the creek,' Jessica said quickly. 'We don't have to go near the tree house.'

Mel shivered. 'I wouldn't go near it if you paid me a hundred dollars.'

'Me neither,' Jessica agreed.

Lauren didn't know what to say. She

didn't believe in ghosts but Mel and
Jessica seemed genuinely scared. What *was*
this tree house like?

After school, Lauren groomed Twilight.
As she worked she told him about the
ride to the creek. 'It will be lovely,' she
said, stopping to wipe her arm across her
hot forehead. 'You'll be able to go into
the water to paddle and drink.'

Twilight nuzzled her shoulder.
Although he couldn't talk back when he
was in his pony form, Lauren knew that
he understood every word she said.

Just then, Max came running down
the path from the house. He seemed to
have forgotten about his nightmare and

was his usual happy, boisterous self. 'Hi, Lauren!' he shouted.

'Where's Buddy?' Lauren asked, surprised to see Max without his puppy.

'Inside,' Max told her, stopping near Twilight and patting him. 'He just wants to lie down. Mum says it's too hot for him outside.'

'Poor Buddy,' Lauren said, thinking of the puppy's thick black fur. 'I bet he wishes he could take his coat off when the weather's like this.'

Max nodded. 'Are you going out for a ride?' he asked.

Lauren nodded. 'I'm going to the creek with Mel and Jessica.'

'Can I come?' Max said.

Lauren hesitated. She really wanted to go with just her friends, but it wouldn't be very nice for Max to be stuck at home on his own.

'*Pleeease*,' Max begged.

'OK,' Lauren agreed. 'You can come on your bike – if Mum says it's all right.'

'Cool!' Max said. 'I'll go and ask.' He turned to run back up the path and then stopped. 'You're not going near that haunted tree house, are you?' he asked, suddenly looking anxious.

Lauren saw the worry in his eyes. 'No, don't worry, we won't,' she said. 'Though there's nothing to be scared of anyway. Ghosts don't exist, you know.'

'I bet they do,' Max said.

'Well, I bet they don't,' Lauren said firmly. She took Twilight's bridle off the fence. 'Now, are you going to ask Mum if you can come? Or shall I go without you?'

'Hold on! I'll go and ask!' Max said, turning to run up the path.

A little while later, Lauren, Mel, Jessica and Max made their way down through the shady woods to Silver Creek. Jessica and Max were cycling ahead on their bikes, while Lauren and Mel rode behind. Occasionally, Twilight would touch noses with Mel's dapple-grey pony, Shadow, as they walked. The two ponies were very good friends.

'This is fun,' Lauren said happily to Mel, as they rode along the sandy trail. Mel nodded and Lauren called out, 'Jessica! Wait and we'll swap – you can ride Twilight the rest of the way to the creek.'

'And you can share Shadow with me on the way back,' Mel offered.

Jessica and Max waited for them to catch up.

Lauren halted Twilight. 'Why don't we go down that track?' she said, nodding towards a small overgrown path that headed off the main trail in the direction of the creek. 'It looks like a short cut.'

'It is,' Mel said, 'but we can't go down there. It goes past the tree house.'

Lauren saw Max gulp. She looked down the shadowy track with its canopy of overhanging trees and saw a tree house up in the branches of an oak tree. It was made of wood and had windows and a roof. It looked as if it would be a wonderful place for a den – from inside you'd be able to see all around. 'It doesn't look haunted to me,' she said.

'Well, it is,' Jessica said. 'And there's no way I'm going down there.'

Max started pushing his bike away from the path. He looked frightened. 'I don't like it here, Lauren. I think there are ghosts.'

'There aren't,' Lauren told him.

Twilight stepped towards the path. His

ears were pricked up and Lauren took courage. If Twilight wasn't scared, then why should she be? She had an idea. 'Watch,' she said to Max. 'I'm going to ride to the tree house and back, just to prove there aren't any ghosts there.'

'Lauren! No!' Mel and Jessica exclaimed.

Lauren ignored them. Touching her heels to Twilight's sides, she rode him down the overgrown path. As they got nearer, the tree house seemed to loom up in front of them. Its old grey walls were covered with green moss and the air around it seemed still and silent. A shiver ran down Lauren's spine. It did look kind of spooky. Her heart started to beat faster.

It couldn't really be haunted, could it?

Seeming to sense her sudden nervousness, Twilight hesitated, his ears flicking back uncertainly.

'Walk on, boy,' Lauren encouraged, but her voice shook slightly. They were very close to the tree house now. She took a deep breath. Just a few more paces and then she'd be able to turn round and Max would see that there was nothing to be frightened of.

'Whooo-aaaaaooooo.' A low noise suddenly groaned through the quiet air.

CHAPTER
Three

Lauren gasped. Twilight stopped dead. The noise was coming from the tree house!

Suddenly something exploded out of the bushes in front of them.

For a moment, all Lauren could see was Twilight's grey mane and neck as he reared in surprise. Behind her, she heard screams. She cried out in alarm, but as

Twilight landed,
her cry turned to
a gasp of relief.
A cat was
streaking
away through
the trees, its ears
flat and its long brown tail flying out
behind it.

Lauren laughed shakily and patted
Twilight's neck. 'It was just a cat,' she said.
She turned in the saddle. Mel, Jessica and
Max were looking rather sheepish.

'I almost fainted with fright,' Jessica
called, as Lauren rode back towards them.

'Me too,' Mel said. 'I was sure it was a
ghost.'

'It could have been a ghost cat,' Max
put in, looking warily into the trees.

'Max,' Lauren said, getting off Twilight,
'how many times do I have to tell you,
there are no such things as ghosts!'

But as she held the stirrup so that
Jessica could mount, she felt a flicker of
doubt. The tree house really had looked
very creepy . . . and what about that
noise? It hadn't sounded like any animal
or bird Lauren had ever heard. Deciding
not to say anything about it in case Max
got even more scared, Lauren picked up
Jessica's bike.

'You were really brave, Lauren,' Max
said, looking at her with respect, as they
cycled on ahead of Mel and Jessica.

'There wasn't anything to be scared of,' Lauren told him as firmly as she could. As his bike wobbled over a tree root, she caught sight of something blue sticking out of the bag on the back of his bike. 'Is that Donkey?' she said in surprise.

Donkey was Max's oldest stuffed toy. He was a faded dark-blue colour with droopy ears. When Max had been little he had taken Donkey everywhere with him, but in the last year he had started to say that Donkey was babyish. Although, as Mrs Foster had told Lauren, this didn't stop Max from taking Donkey to bed with him each night.

Max looked round and, when he saw

Donkey's leg sticking out of his bike bag,
his cheeks turned pink. 'I didn't put him
there,' he said defensively. Quickly he
stopped and pushed Donkey into the
bag. 'Only little kids have cuddly toys.'

Standing up on his pedals, he rode on.

Lauren smiled to herself. Max would never admit it, but she had a feeling that he had brought Donkey along with him just in case they met any ghosts.

They turned down the track that led to the creek. Lauren was warm from cycling and couldn't wait to take her trainers off to wade in the cool water. There were several people there already – some sitting on the grassy banks, others splashing in the sparkling creek.

'Let's go down to the left where it's less busy,' Mel called. They rode to a quiet spot and dismounted from the bikes and ponies.

'Thanks for letting me ride Twilight,'

Jessica said, dismounting. She helped
Lauren run up the stirrups and loosen
Twilight's girth, and then Lauren led
him down to the water.

Twilight walked in up to his knees
and buried his muzzle in the creek. As
he drank the cool, fresh water, Lauren
thought about that evening when they
would go flying through the sky.

After Twilight had been for a paddle,
Lauren led him out of the river and
tied him up to graze with Shadow.
Then she sat down to take her trainers
off. Mel, Jessica and Max were already
down at the water's edge. Leaving her
shoes beside theirs, Lauren went to
join them.

Jessica had brought a ball and they threw it to one another. Then they took it in turns to try skimming stones across the surface of the water.

'This is great,' Max said, turning a smiling face to Lauren's as he hunted for a flat stone. Behind them, Twilight whinnied.

Lauren glanced round, and saw that the three boys from school who had knocked Jessica over were standing by the pile of shoes. They were nudging each other and laughing. Lauren saw the tallest, strongest one, Nick, reach down and pick up the shoes and pass them to Andrew and Dan. They were going to take them!

'Hey!' Lauren shouted, starting to run up the slope towards them.

The boys looked up but, seeing that it was just Lauren, they stood their ground.

Lauren came to a panting stop. 'Leave our shoes alone!'

Andrew, a stocky boy with close-cropped, curly blond hair, grinned and dangled one of Lauren's trainers from his hands. 'Seems to me like you'd have a hard time getting home without them,' he smirked.

'Give them back!' Lauren said.

To her relief, she heard Mel, Jessica and Max running up behind her. They had realized what was happening. 'Give us our shoes!' Jessica exclaimed.

'You'd better ask nicely,' Dan taunted her.

'Hey, what's that?' Nick said, his sharp eyes spotting Donkey's head sticking out of Max's bike bag. The toy had half fallen out when Max had thrown his bike on the ground. Nick swooped down and grabbed Donkey, hauling him out and holding him by his tail. 'Look! It's a stuffed toy!'

Lauren stiffened as she saw poor old Donkey dangling from Nick's huge hand. Only the fact that Nick was head and shoulders taller than she was stopped her from throwing herself at him. 'Put him down,' she said through gritted teeth.

'Yours, is he?' Nick said. His eyes swept

across the group. 'Or maybe he's yours?'
he sneered at Max.

'He's not mine,' Max said, his face
flushing crimson.

'Just give him back,' Lauren said.

'Make me,' Nick taunted.

Lauren lost her temper. Running
towards Nick, she grabbed at Donkey.

With a whoop of delight, Nick
whipped Donkey out of her reach and
then charged away. 'Come and get him if
you want him!'

Dropping the shoes as they went,
Andrew and Dan raced after him along
the bank. Lauren sprinted after them, the
sight of Donkey bouncing around in
Nick's fist spurring her on.

Suddenly the boys stopped. 'Still want him?' Nick called.

'Yes!' Lauren panted as she reached them, and then she realized where they were standing. Just behind them, a little way up an overgrown track, was the tree house!

'Go and get him then,' Nick laughed. Lifting his arm, he hurled Donkey towards the trees. Laughing loudly, he and the other two boys ran away along the bank of the creek.

Lauren stared in horror as Donkey went spinning up into the blue sky, turning over and over until he landed in the branches of a tree . . . right next to the creepy old tree house.

CHAPTER

Four

'Donkey!' Max exclaimed, running up behind Lauren.

'Don't worry,' Lauren said quickly. 'We'll get him down.'

Just then, Mel and Jessica reached them. 'We've got all our shoes,' Mel said. She looked up at the tree. 'Oh.'

'Was he a special toy?' Jessica asked, looking at Max.

Max stared at Donkey for a moment and then he shook his head. 'No,' he said, his voice trembling. 'It's just a silly old thing.' Swinging round, he marched away, but not before Lauren had seen the tears springing to his eyes.

'Max,' Lauren said, going after him and stopping him, 'come on. I'll get Donkey down for you.'

'I don't want him,' Max said angrily, pulling away from her, and he ran down to the creek.

'Maybe we could climb the tree and get it,' Jessica said, joining Lauren. 'But it is very high up.'

'It's OK,' Lauren said quickly, catching Jessica's worried look at the tree house.

'Max says it doesn't matter.' But inside she was thinking, *Tonight Twilight and I can fly here. We can get Donkey down*. For a second, an image of the tree house at night – dark, spooky, surrounded by trees – filled her mind, but she forced it away. She'd be fine with Twilight. They could just swoop down and get Donkey back and then fly away.

Feeling happier, she smiled at Mel and Jessica. They were looking concerned. 'Come on,' she said. 'Let's get back to the ponies.'

That night, while her mum and dad were watching a film on TV, Lauren went out to Twilight's paddock and said the spell that turned him into a unicorn. There was a bright purple flash and suddenly Twilight was standing in front of her – a snow-white unicorn.

'Hello,' he said, nuzzling her. 'Are we going to go and get Max's toy?' Lauren had told him all about her plans for rescuing Donkey while riding back from Mel's.

'Definitely,' Lauren replied. She had heard her mum asking where Donkey was when Max got into bed that evening. Max had replied that he didn't know. He had muttered it as if he didn't care but Lauren was sure that it did matter. Although he'd never admit it, she knew Max loved Donkey almost as much as he loved Buddy.

Grabbing hold of Twilight's mane, Lauren mounted. 'Let's go.'

Twilight leapt up into the sky. 'Twilight,' Lauren said, 'you don't think the tree house is really haunted, do you?'

'I don't know,' Twilight replied.

As the darkness closed in around them, Lauren felt goosebumps prickle her skin. 'But ghosts don't exist,' she said, trying to convince herself by speaking out loud. 'They're just make believe, like monsters or dragons or . . .' Her voice trailed off.

Or unicorns, she thought. She swallowed, her stomach feeling as if it had just done a loop-the-loop. People said unicorns didn't exist, but they did, didn't they? What if she was wrong about ghosts?

Just then her thoughts were distracted by the sight of someone walking in the woods below. Lauren stiffened in surprise. Normally they didn't come across anyone at night. 'Careful!' she whispered quickly to Twilight. 'Look!'

Twilight started to swoop upwards but, as he did so, Lauren recognized the figure below.

'Mrs Fontana!' she exclaimed. 'What are you doing here?' she asked as Twilight cantered downwards and landed beside the old lady.

Mrs Fontana's bright blue eyes

twinkled. 'Walking Walter, of course,' she
said. She whistled softly and Walter, her
little black and white terrier dog, came
bounding out from the bushes. Twilight
lowered his head in greeting. Trotting

over to the unicorn, Walter licked
Twilight on the nose and woofed, before
going to sit at Mrs Fontana's side.

'He says it is good to see you,' Mrs
Fontana said. Her face creased into what
seemed like a hundred wrinkles as she
smiled. 'And he's right – it is. What are
you both up to tonight?' she asked.

'We're going to get my brother's toy,'
Lauren replied. 'Some boys threw it up
into a tree.'

Mrs Fontana nodded, looking pleased.
'So, you're still doing good things then?'

Lauren nodded. Ever since she had
turned Twilight into a unicorn, they had
been secretly helping several of her
friends overcome problems – although, of

course, her friends knew nothing about
the magical side of Twilight. That was the
thing about unicorns – they roamed the
human world looking just like little grey
ponies until they found a Unicorn Friend
– a child with enough imagination to
believe in magic. Once the Turning Spell
had been said and the unicorn had
changed into their magical form, then
they and their Unicorn Friend worked
together, helping others.

'That's as it should be,' Mrs Fontana
said. 'My unicorn and I did a lot of good
too.'

'What happened to your unicorn?'
Lauren asked, remembering her own
conversation with Twilight from the night

before. 'Did he . . . did he die?' Her voice faltered on the words as she imagined how she would feel if Twilight ever died. She was relieved when Mrs Fontana smiled.

'Oh no,' the old lady replied. 'He returned to Arcadia – like all unicorns do.'

Lauren and Twilight stared at her, not quite understanding.

'Unicorns come to this world to carry out good deeds,' Mrs Fontana explained. 'Then they go back to Arcadia – the magical world where they were born. Those unicorns who have been the most courageous and resourceful earn the right to become Golden Unicorns, the wise rulers of Arcadia. That's why you two have to work out how to use Twilight's magical powers all by yourselves,' she said. 'It's a test for Twilight — being here. If he does enough good work, then maybe he will become a Golden Unicorn one day.'

Lauren gripped Twilight's mane. He was going to go away one day? But he couldn't. He was hers.

Twilight seemed to be thinking the same thing. He stamped his foot in alarm. 'But I don't want to go back to Arcadia! I want to stay here with Lauren!'

'One day you will feel differently,' Mrs Fontana said. 'It is your destiny.' Seeing the alarm and unhappiness on their faces,

she shook her head in a kindly way. 'Do
not worry about this now. Concentrate
on being here together.' She smiled.

'Now, my dears, I must go. Come, Walter,'
she said to the little dog.

Walter leapt to his feet, and he and
Mrs Fontana vanished among the trees.

felt when flying. At the back of her
a thought was trying to turn its
words. Lauren tried to catch
she was sure it was impo
had something to do
Fontana had just
'We're her
they reach
Max's

breath. 'We should get Donkey,' she said quietly. 'It's getting late.'

Twilight nodded. Without saying a word, he took off into the sky. But Lauren didn't feel any of the usual joy she

mind,

elf into

hold of it –

rtant and that it

with what Mrs

said.

,' Twilight announced as

ed the creek. 'We should get

toy.'

Lauren took a deep breath and agreed.
After all, she and Twilight were supposed
to do good, just as Mrs Fontana had said.
The old lady's words came back to her:
*Unicorns come to this world to carry out good
deeds and then they go back to Arcadia.*

The thought that had been hovering
vaguely in Lauren's mind suddenly

became clear.

'Twilight!' she gasped, as he rose upwards. 'Stop!'

Halfway to the treehouse, Twilight stopped and hovered in the air. 'What is it?'

'Don't you see?' Lauren said. 'The more good we do, the sooner you'll go away.'

'I don't understand,' Twilight said.

'Mrs Fontana said that you were here to pass a test,' Lauren said. 'To pass it you help others with me. That must mean that when we've done enough good deeds, you'll go back to Arcadia.'

Twilight spoke slowly. 'So, you mean the more I help, the sooner the time comes for me to go away?'

'Yes,' Lauren whispered.

There was a long pause.

Lauren looked at Donkey hanging in the tree and bit her lip. 'You know,

maybe Max doesn't really want Donkey back,' she said suddenly.

He does, a voice inside her head protested. Lauren tried not to listen to it.

'I mean, he *did* say that he thought Donkey was babyish,' she went on out loud, 'and that he didn't want him any more.'

Her mind filled with a picture of Max's face when he had first seen Donkey in the tree. She pushed it away.

'And he's right,' she went on. 'It is kind of babyish for a six-year-old to still take a cuddly animal to bed.'

'So, you think that maybe we *shouldn't* get the toy,' Twilight said hesitantly.

'Yes,' Lauren said. A horrid guilty

feeling was welling up inside her, but she ignored it. 'Let's leave Donkey here.'

'Are you sure?' Twilight asked.

'Definitely,' Lauren said. 'Let's go home.'

But inside she was far from sure.

They flew back to Granger's Farm in silence.

'Goodnight,' Lauren said, after she'd changed Twilight back into a pony. 'I'll see you in the morning.'

Twilight nodded, but Lauren was sure his eyes looked troubled.

We've done the right thing, Lauren told herself as she walked back to the house. *Max didn't really want Donkey.*

And you didn't want to do a good deed

*with Twilight in case it brought him closer to
going away,* the little voice in her head
said.

'That's not true,' Lauren said aloud,
wishing that the little voice would leave
her alone.

On the way up to her bedroom, she
looked into the lounge where her mum
was reading and her dad was watching
the TV.

'I'm going up to bed,' she said.

Her dad looked at the clock on the
wall. 'Have you been with Twilight all this
time?' he asked in surprise.

'Yes,' Lauren replied.

'But it's dark outside,' her mum said.
'What have you been doing?'

Lauren shrugged vaguely. 'Talking to him – this and that.'

Her dad shook his head. 'You know, I thought that maybe you'd lose interest in ponies once you had one of your own, Lauren Foster. But you've sure proved me wrong.'

Her mum smiled. 'You really love that pony, don't you, Lauren?'

Lauren nodded. 'Yes,' she said, 'I do.' She imagined Twilight leaving her and her heart felt as if it was going to break.

Feeling tears spring to her eyes, she rubbed her hand across her face, pretending that she was tired so that her mum and dad wouldn't see. Her mum

came over and kissed her. 'You look
exhausted, honey. Go and get ready for
bed. I'll be up shortly to say goodnight.'

Lauren didn't sleep well that night. She
tossed and turned in her bed – one
minute thinking about Twilight going
away, and the next thinking about
Donkey still hanging in the tree.

  She woke up early and got dressed.
On the way downstairs she passed Max's
room. Max wasn't in his bed. Wondering
where he was, Lauren carried on. The
door to her mum and dad's room was
open and when Lauren looked in she
saw that Max was in their parents' bed.
Her dad had already got up and had

started work on the farm. Lauren stopped in the doorway.

Mrs Foster opened her eyes. 'Hi, there,' she said, sitting up in bed. She glanced at the bedside clock. 'You're up early.'

'I was having bad dreams,' Lauren told her.

'Not you as well,' Mrs Foster said, yawning. 'Max had another nightmare last night too.'

Just then Max woke up. 'Mummy?'

'I'm here,' Mrs Foster said, kissing his dark head.

'I like sleeping in your bed,' Max said to her, cuddling closer.

'Well, I'm afraid that tonight it's back to your own bed,' Mrs Foster said.

'There's hardly any space for your dad
and me with you in here as well.'

'But my bed's lonely,' Max said.

Mrs Foster ruffled his hair. 'It won't be

when we find Donkey. I'll have a look for
him today.'

Max's eyes met Lauren's. *So*, she
realized, *he hasn't told Mum where Donkey
really is.*

'I don't need Donkey,' Max muttered.

'Well, maybe I'll try and find him
anyway,' Mrs Foster said, smiling at
Lauren.

Max saw the smile and threw the
covers back. 'You won't be able to,' he
said, getting up. 'And, anyway, it doesn't
matter. I told you – I don't care.' But as
he pushed past Lauren, she saw the
unhappiness in his eyes.

Lauren felt dreadful all day. *I should have*

got Donkey down from the tree for Max, she thought as she stared unseeingly at a page of sums at school. It was just . . .

She swallowed as she admitted the truth. It was just that if she and Twilight did good deeds, then Twilight would have to leave her.

Mel leaned over. 'You OK, Lauren?' she asked.

'I'm fine,' Lauren said, trying to smile.

But inside, she knew that she wasn't fine at all.

CHAPTER

Six

'I don't want to go to bed,' Max said,
clinging to Mrs Foster's arm that
evening when she suggested that it was
his bedtime. 'Can't I stay up – please,
Mum?'

'No,' Mrs Foster said, looking at his
pale face. 'You look worn out. Come on
– upstairs with you. You can snuggle
down in bed and I'll read you a story.'

Max hung back. Mrs Foster crouched down beside him. 'Hey, how about just for one night, we let Buddy sleep in your room with you?' she said. 'Will that make you feel better?'

Max nodded. 'Yes.'

'OK then,' Mrs Foster said kindly. 'Just this once. Come on, Buddy,' she said to the puppy, who was stretched out on the floor in front of the sofa. 'You can come upstairs.'

Buddy leapt to his feet. Wagging his tail, he bounded towards the door, stopping to give Max a slobbery lick on the way. Looking a bit happier, Max headed for the stairs with Mrs Foster.

Lauren followed them. Sitting down in her room to do her homework, she could hear her mum settling Max in his bed and starting to read to him.

Mrs Foster read on for what seemed a long time. It wasn't until Lauren had started on the last of her homework –

spellings – that she heard her mum turn
the light off and quietly leave Max's
room.

'Mum!' It was Max's voice.

Through her half-open door, Lauren
saw her mum pause in Max's doorway,
her face looking tired. 'Yes, Max?'

'I . . .' Max seemed to be struggling
with the words. 'I want Donkey.'

Lauren's heart clenched.

'I'm sorry, honey,' Mrs Foster said
gently. 'But I just don't know where he
is. Cuddle your other toys instead. We can
have another look in the morning.'

She waited a moment by the door.
When Max said no more, she turned and
went downstairs.

Lauren looked at the printed column of spellings in her school book with its red and gold logo, but she couldn't concentrate on them. After a while, she went to her brother's bedroom. 'Max?' she whispered. There was no answer. Maybe he'd fallen asleep.

Lauren pushed the door open. 'Max?' she whispered again.

And then she heard the sound of Max crying quietly.

'Oh, Max!' Lauren exclaimed. She ran to his bed. Max was lying face down, crying into his pillow. Buddy was sitting beside him, whimpering anxiously. Crouching down, Lauren put her arms round her little brother. 'Max, please

don't cry.'

Through the darkness, Max lifted a
tear-stained face to hers. 'I miss Donkey,
Lauren.'

The words tumbled out of Lauren. 'I'll

get him for you,' she said.

Max sat up in bed and stroked Buddy's head. 'You can't. He's too high up in that tree and it's right by the haunted tree house.' He gulped and Buddy reached up to lick the salty tears from his cheeks with his pink tongue. 'He's gone forever.'

'He hasn't,' Lauren told him. 'I'll get him. I promise.'

'Really?' Max said, a faint light of hope glimmering in his eyes.

Lauren nodded. 'Really,' she answered.

Leaving Max with Buddy, Lauren went downstairs. 'I'm just going to see Twilight,' she said to her mum and dad, who were in the kitchen.

'Don't be out too long,' her dad said. 'It'll be dark soon.'

'Have you done your homework?' Mrs Foster asked.

Lauren nodded. She still had the spellings to learn but she could look over them the next morning.

'OK then,' her mum said.

Lauren pulled on her trainers and hurried outside. As she reached the path that led to Twilight's paddock, she started to run.

Hearing the sound of her footsteps, Twilight came trotting to the gate.

'Twilight,' Lauren said quickly. 'We've got to go out flying.'

Twilight whinnied and Lauren said the

words of the Turning Spell.

'What's happened?' he asked.

'Max is really upset about Donkey,'
Lauren said. 'He can't sleep. I feel awful.'
She stepped forward and stroked his
neck. 'Twilight, even if it does mean that
it brings the time closer when you have
to go away, we've got to get Donkey
back. I just can't let my brother be so
upset.'

'Of course you can't,' Twilight said.
'We must help.' He shook his mane. 'It
was strange yesterday when we didn't get
Max's toy. It somehow felt wrong. But
this,' he nuzzled her, 'this feels right.'

'I know,' Lauren replied with a smile.

★

They flew to
the creek
and landed
on the
grassy bank.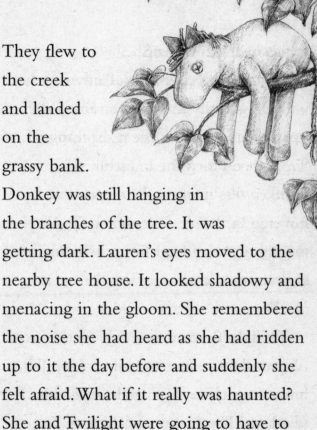
Donkey was still hanging in
the branches of the tree. It was
getting dark. Lauren's eyes moved to the
nearby tree house. It looked shadowy and
menacing in the gloom. She remembered
the noise she had heard as she had ridden
up to it the day before and suddenly she
felt afraid. What if it really was haunted?
She and Twilight were going to have to
fly right beside it to get Donkey.

Trying not to feel scared, Lauren
patted Twilight's neck. 'OK,' she

whispered. 'Let's fly up.'

Twilight leapt upwards. Lauren's heart was pounding but she felt strong – she knew she was doing the right thing. As Twilight reached the branches where Donkey was hanging, he stopped and hovered in the air. Untangling Donkey's woolly mane and tail from the branches, Lauren took him safely into her arms.

'I've got him!' she cried.

Twilight flew on upwards. As they rose up past the tree house, Lauren even felt brave enough to look in through the windows. The moon was shining through one of them, lighting up the inside of the wooden house. There was nothing there. It was empty. Well, apart

from some rubbish on the wooden floorboards – chocolate wrappers, empty cans, a comic and a . . .

'Twilight – stop,' Lauren said suddenly.

'What's the matter?' Twilight asked.

'Can you take me close to one of the windows, please?' Lauren asked.

'Sure.' Twilight did as she asked. Lauren looked in again. Yes, there on the floor of the tree house was a school spelling book with a red and gold logo. It was from Lauren's school! But what was it doing in the tree house?

She also realized that the rubbish on the floor looked new. The discarded wrappers were still bright and colourful and the comic was the latest issue of

Spider-man – Lauren had seen some of
the kids in her class reading similar copies
only the day before.

But who would have been in the tree
house? Everyone was scared of it.

Lauren looked at the spelling book
again and made up her mind. 'I have to
go inside,' she said to Twilight.

'OK,' Twilight said, flying as close to
the window as he could.

The wood of the tree house was old
but solid. As Lauren grabbed hold of the
window sill and pulled herself over it,
she found herself thinking again that it
would make a wonderful den. It was so
lovely up in the tree and in the daytime
you must be able to see all around.

She saw something white in one
corner and stopped. It looked like a pile
of cotton sheets. Her skin prickled. What
if there was something under them?

Taking a deep breath, she crept over
and touched the edge of the sheet with
the toe of her trainer. Nothing moved.
Lauren moved the top sheet. Underneath
it there were two more sheets, a toy
microphone and a long stick.

Lauren frowned and picked up the
microphone. Max had one like it at
home. It made your voice sound strange
and echoey when you spoke into it. But
what was it doing here?

She walked over to the school book and
opened it curiously. Who did it belong to?

A name was written inside.

Lauren gasped. *Nick Snyder.* He was the
boy who had thrown Donkey into the
tree. But what had he been doing in the
tree house?

Her eyes widened. There was only one explanation. 'Twilight,' she said, hurrying to the window. 'I think the boys who threw Donkey into the tree are trying to pretend the place is haunted!'

'What?' Twilight snorted in surprise.

'There's a school book on the floor that belongs to one of them,' Lauren told him quickly. 'So they must have been here. There are some sheets and a stick. You could hang the sheets on a stick and wave them high up in the branches to make people think they've seen ghosts. There's also a toy microphone. I bet the boys have been using it to make that spooky noise we heard.'

'But why would they do that?'

Twilight asked in astonishment.

'I don't know,' Lauren said. She started to climb over the window ledge and on to his back. 'But I think we should try to find out.'

CHAPTER
Seven

As Lauren went up to her bedroom, she stopped by Max's door. 'Max,' she said softly.

There was only the sound of Max's breathing. He had finally fallen asleep.

Lauren went quietly into the room. Buddy was lying beside the bed. He thumped his tail on the floor when he saw Lauren, but he didn't get up.

Lauren tucked Donkey under Max's arm. "Night, Buddy,' she whispered and then, with a smile, she crept out of the room.

At six o'clock in the morning, Max came flying into her room with Donkey in his arms. 'Lauren!' he cried, jumping on to her bed and waking her with a start. 'You got Donkey back for me!'

Lauren grinned. 'I told you I would.'

'But how?' Max said.

Lauren decided it was best to tell him part of the truth. She lowered her voice. 'I used magic,' she whispered.

Max didn't quite seem able to decide whether to believe her. 'Really?'

Lauren nodded.

'Wow!' Max gasped, his eyes widening.

'But you can't tell anyone,' Lauren whispered quickly. 'If Mum asks where Donkey was, just tell her that you found him under the bed or something.'

'OK,' Max agreed eagerly. He sat down on the bed. 'What sort of magic was it, Lauren?'

'I can't tell you,' Lauren smiled. 'It's a secret kind of magic.'

'Please tell me,' Max begged.

Lauren shook her head.

'But . . .'

'Max!' Lauren exclaimed and, picking up one of the cuddly toys from the end of her bed, she hit him with it. 'I said it's a secret!'

Max hit her back with Donkey and the next minute they were in the middle of a toy fight, gasping with laughter as they fell about on Lauren's bed.

At school that day, Lauren watched Nick and his friends. During break they hung out together, muscling in on a game that some of the younger kids were playing.

Lauren frowned as she watched them. They were so mean.

As she and her mum and Max drove home from school that afternoon, Lauren saw Nick and his friends cycling along the pavement. They were pedalling fast, weaving in and out through the other children. As Lauren watched, they turned down a path that led in the direction of the creek. *And,* Lauren thought, *towards the tree house.*

As soon as Lauren got home, she groomed and saddled Twilight. 'We have to go to the tree house,' she told him. 'I want to see if Nick and his friends are there. But they mustn't see us.'

As they set off into the woods, Twilight pulled eagerly at his bit and Lauren let him trot along the sandy trail. As she rode, she wondered how she could get close to the tree house without the boys seeing.

Suddenly Twilight stopped. He was looking down a little overgrown path to the right, as if he wanted to go that way.

'No, Twilight,' Lauren said. 'We're going to the tree house.'

Twilight stamped his foot.

Lauren frowned. Was he trying to tell her something?

'You think we should go down here? Does this lead to the tree house?'

Twilight nodded.

Lauren touched her heels to his sides and he walked quickly down the path. After a little way, it forked. Lauren left the reins loose on Twilight's neck and he took the right-hand path. They walked on for a minute more, with Lauren dodging the low overhanging branches. Then Twilight came to a halt.

Looking straight ahead, he whickered softly.

Lauren stared. The tree house was just ahead of them, half hidden by trees. If she got off and crawled through the undergrowth she could get to it without having to go down one of the main paths – she could see what the boys were doing without being noticed.

'Clever boy,' she breathed, giving Twilight a hug.

Twilight snorted. Lauren dismounted and began to creep through the thick green undergrowth towards the tree house.

As she got closer she could hear the sound of low voices. Her heart started to

'Go on – I dare you to touch the tree,'
one of them said to the other.

'Sure,' she heard the other reply rather
nervously. 'But it's not really haunted.'

And then, seemingly from the air,
came a disembodied groaning noise.
Lauren knew exactly what was making
the noise – one of the boys with the toy

microphone. She could have laughed out loud at how simple it was, but it wasn't funny.

The two girls screamed and raced back to the creek.

From the tree house came the muffled sounds of laughter.

'That was great!' Lauren heard Dan say.

'They were so scared,' Nick said. 'It's perfect. If I hadn't thought of this, then we'd have had to share this place.'

He sounded very pleased with himself and Lauren felt a wave of anger. Little kids were having nightmares about ghosts and it was all because three boys were too selfish to share the tree house. It was only the thought that

the three of them were so much bigger
than she was that stopped her from
climbing up there and telling them what
she thought of them.

Instead, she crawled back to Twilight.

She didn't say anything until they had
moved out of sight of the tree house, and
then she told him what she had heard.

'Can you believe them?' she demanded
indignantly. 'Of all the dumb things to
do!' Twilight shook his head. Lauren
longed for him to be able to answer back
but she couldn't risk turning him into a
unicorn in broad daylight in case
someone saw. Instead, she stroked his
neck. 'We've got to do something about
them.'

She thought hard. The question was —
what?

After supper, Lauren left the house and,
in the gathering dusk, turned Twilight
into a unicorn.

'What are we going to do about those
boys?' Twilight said immediately.

'I don't know,' Lauren said. She'd been
wracking her brains.

'We should scare them just like they've
been scaring everyone else,' Twilight said.

'But how?' Lauren asked.

'I'm not sure,' Twilight admitted with a
snort.

Lauren remembered a bit of the boys'
conversation. 'They said they were going

to stay at the tree house tonight. Let's go there now. Maybe we could make noises in the bushes or something – that might scare them.' She wasn't convinced it would work but she desperately wanted to do something, and fast.

Twilight nodded. Lauren climbed on to his back and they cantered away into the sky.

To Lauren's surprise, the tree house was quiet when they arrived. 'They're not here yet,' she said.

'Listen,' Twilight said. 'They're coming.'

Lauren heard the sound of the boys running along the path from the creek.

'Let's fly higher!' she said quickly.

'They mustn't see us.'

As Twilight rose into the sky, Nick and Andrew came running along the path. They were clutching several bags of sweets and bars of chocolate. Dan was a little way behind, carrying a large bag of drinks cans.

'Wait!' he was saying. 'These drinks are heavy!'

'Come on!' Nick called to Andrew. 'Let's eat everything before Dan gets here!' He shouted it loud enough for Dan to hear.

'Hey!' Dan shouted in protest. 'Wait! That's not fair!'

Nick and Andrew reached the rope ladder. Nick climbed into the tree house

first while Andrew waited. Then Andrew
passed the food and scrambled up the
ladder himself.

Watching from above, Lauren saw

Nick whisper something to Andrew. They both grinned and started to haul up the ladder.

The last rung had just disappeared into the tree house when Dan came panting up the path. 'Put the ladder back down!'

Nick and Andrew looked out, grinning. 'Not till we've eaten all the food!' Nick said.

Then he and Andrew disappeared back into the tree house.

Dan shouted out angrily. 'Come on, guys. Stop messing around. Let me in!'

Neither Nick nor Andrew appeared and it seemed as if they were going to eat all the chocolate and crisps themselves.

Dan looked around. It was getting

darker by the second and Lauren saw an
alarmed expression cross his face. An owl
hooted overhead and she saw him jump.
'This isn't funny any more,' he shouted
up to the boys in the tree house. 'Let
me in.'

Nick's voice floated out through the
windows. 'Scared of the ghosts?' he called.
And he and Andrew cracked up laughing.

His words gave Lauren an idea.
'Twilight! This is our chance!' she said.
'Let's swoop down and frighten Dan.
Make yourself look fierce – point your
horn at him.'

'You mean, let him see me?' Twilight
said in astonishment.

'It's dark. He's alone. No one will

believe him if he says he's seen a
unicorn.' Lauren knew it was risky but
she had a feeling it would work. If they
could frighten Dan, then maybe they
could frighten the other two as well.
'Come on!' she said, grabbing his mane.
'Let's go for it!'

CHAPTER

Eight

With a great whinny, Twilight plunged down from the sky. He galloped through the air towards Dan, his horn pointing at the boy, his dark eyes flashing with fire.

Lauren ducked low on Twilight's back but not before she had caught sight of Dan staring at Twilight in horror. His mouth gaped open.

'*Arghhhhhhhh!*' he yelled in terror, as Twilight bore down on him.

The unicorn swooped upwards, missing him by centimetres, and disappeared into the darkness of the woods. He landed quietly.

Dan was still yelling and now the

other boys were shouting too. There was the sound of the rope ladder being let down. Lauren clutched Twilight's neck, gulping back her laughter as she remembered Dan's horrified face when he had seen Twilight appear out of the sky.

'What's up?' she heard Nick shouting to Dan as he clambered down the ladder.

'It was . . . it came through the sky at me . . . big horn . . . galloping!' Dan shouted.

'What came at you?' Lauren heard Andrew demand.

'It was a uni– ' Dan broke off as if he couldn't believe what he had seen with his own eyes. 'It was a horse,' he said quickly. 'A great white flying horse.'

'A flying horse!' Nick and Andrew exclaimed.

'With someone riding it,' Dan gasped. 'It came out of the sky. It just galloped straight at me. I couldn't see the person's head. Just their legs.'

'You mean a headless horseman?' Andrew laughed. 'Like a ghost!'

'Yeah!' Dan said, agreeing quickly. 'Yeah, that's what it was – it was a ghost!'

Nick and Andrew both laughed loudly.

'As if,' Nick said.

An idea filled Lauren's mind. 'Gallop round!' she said to Twilight. 'Make the sound of hoofbeats. Let's make them think there really *is* a headless horseman!'

Twilight didn't need telling twice.

Pricking up his ears, he started to canter through the bushes around the tree house, stamping his feet down as hard as he could.

'Listen!' Dan cried. 'There it is again!'

'Hey, you're right. I can see it!' Nick said, suddenly sounding frightened. 'Look – it's moving through the trees.'

'I can see it too!' cried Andrew.

Whinnying loudly, Twilight started cantering directly for the tree house. The sound of his hoofbeats seemed to fill the forest as he galloped down the path.

'*Arghhhhhhh!*' all three boys shouted in fright. 'It's a ghost – a real ghost!' And the next minute, Lauren saw them running off through the woods, falling over tree roots and stumbling over stones in their panic. Still yelling, they disappeared out of sight.

Twilight stopped. 'We did it!'

Lauren's face split in a grin of astonishment and delight. They'd actually scared the boys away.

Twilight tossed his mane proudly. 'I must have looked really frightening.'

'I reckon you did,' Lauren smiled, hugging him. 'You were great.'

'It was your idea,' Twilight said.

'They were so scared,' Lauren laughed. 'Serves them right.'

Twilight snorted in a way that made it sound very much as if he was laughing too. 'Somehow I don't think they'll be coming back here in a hurry.'

Lauren patted his neck. 'I think you're right. Come on, let's go.'

As Twilight rose into the sky, Lauren frowned. 'I wonder if Nick's spelling book is still in the tree house,' she said. 'He'll get into trouble if he goes to school and says he's lost it.'

Part of her thought that Nick Snyder deserved all the trouble he got, but then she told herself not to be mean. He'd had enough of a fright without getting into trouble at school as well. 'Let's find it for him,' she said.

Twilight flew to the window. 'You know,' Lauren said, as she climbed inside to get Nick's book, 'this is going to make a great place for everyone to come and play. Now the boys have left it, everyone will be able to use it.' She reappeared with Nick's school book.

'So it looks like we've done two good deeds, after all,' Twilight said.

Lauren paused on the window ledge. 'I guess we have.'

They looked at each other. Neither of them spoke, but Lauren was sure she knew what Twilight was thinking. Had they just brought the time when he was going to leave her even closer?

The happiness that had been fizzing through her suddenly faded away.

She climbed slowly on to his back and they set off in an unhappy silence.

They were almost back at Granger's Farm when Lauren saw someone in the woods. 'It's Mrs Fontana and

Walter,' she said.

Twilight landed beside the old lady and the terrier.

'Hello again,' Mrs Fontana said, smiling at them. 'Where have you two been?'

'We've been at the creek scaring away some boys who'd been pretending the tree house was haunted,' Lauren replied in a subdued voice.

Mrs Fontana noticed her sadness. 'What's the matter? You don't sound very happy.'

Lauren looked at the ground. Twilight hung his head.

'What is it?' Mrs Fontana said with concern.

The words came tumbling out of Lauren's mouth. 'Oh, Mrs Fontana,' she answered unhappily, 'I don't know what to do. The more we help people, the sooner Twilight will have to go back to Arcadia. I want to do good but I don't want him to leave.'

'But the amount of good you do doesn't affect when Twilight leaves,' Mrs Fontana said in surprise.

'It doesn't?' Lauren said.

'No, my dear,' Mrs Fontana replied, shaking her head. 'You must have misunderstood me. Twilight will be with you for as long as you want him to be. It's up to you when he leaves.'

'I . . . I don't understand,' Lauren stammered in confusion.

Mrs Fontana took hold of her hands.

'One day, you will grow up and no longer need Twilight, Lauren,' she said, her bright eyes looking into Lauren's face. '*That* will be the day when the time has come for Twilight to go – and if he's done enough good deeds, then he'll become a Golden Unicorn.'

'But I'll always need Twilight,' Lauren exclaimed. Her eyes lit up with hope. 'Does that mean he can stay with me forever, Mrs Fontana?'

'He will stay for as long as you need him,' Mrs Fontana repeated softly.

Lauren looked at Twilight with delight. 'Then everything's OK.' She put her arms round his neck and hugged him close. 'You won't ever have to go away,

Twilight.' She turned to Mrs Fontana.
'We'll be together forever!'

A look full of wisdom and sadness
seemed to cross the old lady's face.
'Maybe,' she murmured.

Walter woofed and glanced down the

path. Mrs Fontana smiled and pulled her yellow shawl around her shoulders. 'I must go. Goodnight.'

'Goodnight,' Lauren replied.

Mrs Fontana started to walk away, then paused and looked back. 'The time you have together is precious,' she said softly, her bright eyes flickering intently from Lauren to Twilight. 'Make the most of it, my dears.'

CHAPTER

Nine

'Lauren! Wait for me!'
Lauren turned on her way in
through the school gates the next
morning and saw Mel running towards
her.

'Hi there,' Lauren said, waiting for her.

'Hi!' Mel said. She looked around.
'Where's Max? Isn't he coming to school
today?'

'He's over there,' Lauren said. Max had run on ahead and was already playing ball with his friends. He was laughing and shouting happily.

'Do you want to go for a ride this afternoon?' Mel asked as she and Lauren continued into school.

'Yeah,' Lauren said.

Just then, Nick, Andrew and Dan came cycling past them. Lauren looked at them closely. Their faces were pale.

'Uh-oh,' Mel said, seeing them. 'Max and his friends had better watch out.'

Lauren watched the boys get off their bikes. 'If we go for a ride, we could go down to the creek again,' she said to Mel. She raised her voice so that the boys could hear. 'I want to explore that tree house.'

She saw Mel look at her with astonishment, but her attention was focused on the three boys. At the mention of the words *tree house* they swung round and stared at her.

'The tree house by the creek!' Dan said, looking scared. 'Don't go there – it's haunted!'

'By a headless horseman,' Andrew put in, coming over. 'He was there last night.'

'We saw him,' Dan told them. 'It was horrible!'

Mel's eyes widened with alarm. 'Really?'

'Yeah,' Nick said earnestly. 'I am never

going near that tree house again.' He looked at Lauren. 'I wouldn't go there if I were you.'

'I see,' Lauren said innocently.

The boys started to walk off.

'By the way, Nick,' Lauren called. She rummaged in her bag. 'Is this yours?' As she spoke, she held out Nick's book.

Nick came over. Taking it, he checked the inside cover and then stared at her. 'Yes. How did *you* get it?'

Lauren spoke coolly. 'Oh, I found it when I went to the tree house last night.'

She had to bite back a grin as all three boys and Mel stared at her as if she'd just gone crazy.

'*You* went to the tree house last night?'

Nick exclaimed.

'You couldn't have — we were there until it was dark,' Andrew said.

'I went *after* it was dark,' Lauren said.

'Did you see the headless horseman?' Dan demanded.

'I didn't,' Lauren said. She smiled cheerfully. 'But I promise I'll let you guys know if I see him *next* time I'm there.'

She took Mel's arm and smiled sweetly at them. 'See you then,' she said to the boys and, enjoying the speechless looks on their faces, she pulled Mel away.

Rounding a corner out of sight of the boys, Lauren burst out laughing.

Mel stared at her in astonishment. 'OK,' she said, breaking away and putting her hands on her hips. 'What *is* going on?'

Lauren grinned. 'It's a long story. Let's find Jessica and I'll tell you all about it.'

'I am *so* glad this place isn't haunted,' Jessica said as she, Lauren and Mel made themselves at home in the tree house after school. Below them, Shadow and

Twilight were grazing by the creek.
'Now everyone can share it and have
fun.'

'Yeah,' Mel agreed, looking around
as if she could hardly believe it. 'It'll be
great!' She shook her head. 'So, tell us
again,' she said to Lauren. 'You rode
here and scared Nick and the others by
galloping around on Twilight and
pretending to be a ghost?'

For about the fiftieth time, Lauren
nodded and told the story. 'I heard the
boys here after school talking about
scaring people and I saw them do it. I
knew it wasn't haunted then, so I came
back later with Twilight.' She crossed her
fingers as she stretched the truth slightly.

'I wore a sheet
and pretended to be a ghost. Because
it was dark, Nick and the others
couldn't see Twilight properly through
the trees and they thought I was a real
ghost – a headless horseman.'

'That's incredible!' Jessica said.

'It was really brave of you to come here on your own at night,' Mel said admiringly to Lauren, 'even if you knew this place wasn't haunted.'

Lauren looked out of the window at Twilight grazing below. 'But I wasn't on my own,' she said, smiling. 'I had Twilight.'